BITSY AND THE MYSTERY AT AMELIA ISLAND

VONDA SKINNER SKELTON

An Imprint of The Overmountain Press
JOHNSON CITY, TENNESSEE

Hardcover ISBN 1-57072-306-0
Trade Paper ISBN 1-57072-307-9

Printed in the United States of America

1 2 3 4 5 6 7 8 9 0

For my grandchildren,
Garrett Hunt, Elliott Hunt,
Cole Matheny, and Mallory Matheny.
Here's another story from MaMa.

ACKNOWLEDGMENTS

Although it's the author who puts the words on paper, many people are involved in the book-building process. My gratitude and thanks to:

Pamela Brown for the tour of her lovely home, the Phelan-Verot House, also known as the Nuns' House, and for allowing me to use her pink cockatoo as the model for Mooshew. Your home, along with its history, was the perfect setting for this story.

Rhonda Norhine, Christine Kjellberg, and the helpful staff at the Amelia Island Museum of History. Thank you for the history lesson, and for answering the questions I forgot to ask.

Glenda Kohlenberger, Mike Lyons, and the late Joanna Cornett at Ghost Tours of Amelia Island. This story was born on that July night.

Dickie Anderson for her assistance with setting, and to Robin Burbank and Dee Dee Thornton for their personal Amelia Island tour from a native's point of view.

Richard Whiddon, Bill Freeman, and Johnny Burbank for answers to technical questions; to Officers Ed Gibson and Curtis Stansbury of the Wilmington (North Carolina) Police Department for help with police dog commands; and to Judy Leach of www.mytoos.com for answering my questions about cockatoos. Anything I got right was because of these good people. Anything I missed I did on my own.

Brian Cockman for naming the police dog, Trooper,

and to Jaci Wilkerson for naming the cockatoo, Mooshew. Thanks and congratulations!

My first readers, Katie Capelli, Laurel Cook, Marsha Ferguson, Emily Holcomb, Christina Skelton Hunt, Nicole Skelton Matheny, Blair Newcomer, Ruth Skinner Poole, Hannah Raines, Cathy Strawhorn, Ashley Teague, Corrie VanDyke, Ellis Vidler, and Melissa Williams. Your close attention to detail saved me!

The Monastery of St. Clare in Greenville, South Carolina, and A Snail's Pace in Saluda, North Carolina, for solitary places to write.

Beth, Sherry, Karin, Archer, Vicki, and the rest of the gang at Silver Dagger. I'm so glad we found each other.

My husband, Gary Skelton, for his continued love and support. I couldn't have done it without you. 143!

AUTHOR'S NOTE

This book, set on Amelia Island, Florida, is a work of fiction. All names, characters, places, and events are either the product of the author's imagination or are used fictitiously. Some of the landmarks are accurately placed in their true settings, while others are completely fictional. Any other resemblance to actual events or persons, living or dead, is entirely coincidental and beyond the intent of either the author or the publisher. I hope those familiar with Amelia Island and Fernandina Beach will enjoy reading about both the real and the imagined.

CHAPTER · 1

"OH NO!" ELLIE SAID. SHE GRABBED MY ARM AND dragged me toward the huge magnolia tree. "Come on, Bitsy, we've got to hide!"

I yanked my arm from my friend. "What?"

"Shhh! He'll hear you."

We reached the ivy-covered tree, and Ellie crouched down, making her eleven-year-old body as tiny as possible. "Did he see us?"

I knelt beside her and pulled back a branch of waxy green leaves. "You mean that skinny kid with the spiked hair? The one over there by the cemetery?" I twisted the gold "B" hanging from my necklace.

"Yeah." Ellie nodded, a stray lock of blonde hair falling in her face.

"I don't think he saw us," I said, "but so what if he did?"

She stared past me and barely whispered, "That's Ernie."

I took a second look. "Do you mean—"

"Yep, he's the one. The male half of the demon duo. Believe me, you don't want to mess with him."

I have to admit, when Ellie and her brother, Garrett, first warned me about Ernie Van Tache, I was a little nervous. After all, he was the neighborhood bully. And his twin sister, Bernie, didn't sound much better.

But now that I had seen him, he didn't look so tough. I stood, brushed off my knees, and wrapped a brown curl around my ear.

Ellie frowned. "What are you doing?"

"I'm going to show him I'm not scared of him. I've heard that's the best way to deal with a bully."

"Are you crazy?" Ellie whispered. She grabbed my shirt. "Get down."

By now, Ernie was only a few steps away. I snatched my shirttail back from Ellie. She hunched over, buried her head in her knees, and hugged her arms around her legs.

I straightened my shoulders to full height, stuffed my hands in my pockets, and confidently stepped out from behind the tree. "Hi," I said, real nice-like.

Ernie jumped back and his mouth dropped open. He was surprised. *Good!* I smiled real big.

He didn't say anything. He just studied me, first looking down at my small feet and then up to the top of my head. After a second, his lips curled together and he smirked.

I'd seen that kind of look a bunch of times. Like a lot of other people, he thought I was only a wimpy little girl. He thought he had nothing to fear from me. *Well, he'd better think again.*

I might be short for a twelve-year-old, but everybody knows what they say about small packages. Obviously, Ernie didn't know he was dealing with dynamite.

He crossed his arms over his skinny chest.

I took my hands out of my pockets.

His lips curled again. "Did you say something to me, squirt?"

Ellie whimpered, but I just bit my tongue. Oh, I could think of all kinds of smart-mouth things to say back to him, but I decided this was a good time to try out my new Bible verse. It's in Romans and it says, *As far as it depends on me, I will live at peace with everyone* . . . or something like that.

Sure, I'd rather tell him off, but I really wanted to do the right thing, for once. So I smiled. "Yeah, I said 'hi.' I just wanted to meet you, that's all."

He scrunched his eyebrows. "You what?"

I took in a deep breath and smiled again. I could tell my kindness was starting to work on him. "I just wanted to meet you. I'm staying here on Amelia Island this week with Garrett and Ellie. We're best friends, you know."

"Best friends, huh?"

"Uh-huh. I'm from South Carolina, where they used to live."

"Then how about giving your best friends a message for me."

Hey, this is going pretty good, I thought. "Sure," I said.

Ellie pulled on my shirt and whispered, "Forget it, Bitsy. Let's go!" But I jerked back without even looking at her.

Ernie squinted his hazel eyes until they were tiny slits. "Tell Smelly-Jelly-Belly-Ellie and Garrett-Carrot to keep out of my way, and I might let them live." He crossed his arms even tighter and smirked again.

I glowered back at the bully. "What?"

"You heard me. Hey, what's your name, squirt?"

I took a small step toward him, peered up at his dirty face, and put my hands on my hips. "Bitsy."

"Oh, as in Betsy Wetsy?"

This time I took a giant step right to him, stretched to my tiptoes, and glared up into his beady eyes. "It's Bitsy. B-I-T-S-Y. Now, you take that back."

"Make me, squirt." That's when he pushed me.

I reached up and pushed him back. So much for being nice.

Ernie lost his footing and fell against the big magnolia tree. Before I knew what was happening, he was back on his feet. He grabbed me and threw me down. My elbows and knees scraped the ground, and my right cheek hit against a rock as I landed, hard.

"Bitsy, watch out!" Ellie yelled.

Ernie leaped toward me.

Ellie took off running.

I rolled out of his way at the last second, flipped over, and jumped onto his back. My bloody knees pressed against his white T-shirt as I tried to grab his arms. But he was too strong, and I wasn't heavy enough to keep him down. I tried to hold on to his bloody shirt as he struggled up on all fours, but I lost my balance and fell face-first to the ground. I didn't stay down long. In one continuous motion, I spit the black dirt out of my mouth, jumped to my feet, and put up my fists.

Now that I've had time to think back on it, it was a pretty dumb thing to do. The problem is, I have a hard time admitting when I'm out of my league. And I was definitely out of my league on this one.

Determined not to back down, I kept my dirty fists in the air as I gasped for breath, my eyes locked with his. He glared back at me, huffing and puffing, holding up his own bloody fists. But before either one of us could make the next move, I heard the sound of running feet slapping the pavement. The kids began yelling before they reached us.

"Ernie! You stop right this very minute, or I'm telling Aunt Myrna!"

Grief. This must be Bernie, I thought.

"Bitsy!" Garrett yelled.

Ernie and I both held our positions and continued the stare-down. Within seconds, Bernie jumped between us, facing her brother. Then she whispered to him through clenched teeth, "What do you think you're doing?"

Garrett grabbed my shirt and dragged me back to the tree. "Are you crazy? Don't you know who that is?"

I kept my fists up and faced Garrett.

He gasped. "Bitsy, you're bleeding."

Ellie ran up to us, saw the blood, and screamed at Ernie, "Look what you did to my best friend, you . . . you . . . bully! I'm telling my mom!" She took off back toward the house.

Bernie shoved her twin brother ahead of her. "Now, you get on home and clean yourself up before Aunt Myrna gets there. She's not going to be happy when she sees you looking like this."

As Ernie approached the tree, he slowed and then stopped, glaring at me again. I held my breath and didn't blink, still keeping my fists up. My arms felt like they were going to fall off, but I didn't move a muscle. It seemed to take forever before he turned and headed toward the sidewalk.

Bernie stopped in front of me, her light brown hair dancing around her face. "Not too smart, are you?" she said.

I kept my mouth shut.

Once they got past us, I dropped my fists and started breathing again. "Well," I sputtered, "that wasn't too bad."

"How can you say that?" Garrett asked. "Look at you."

I inspected the damage. My arms were dirty, but it was my elbows that were screaming in pain. I tried to wipe away the blood, but it just smeared into the black dirt covering my arms. Then I saw my knees. Both were scraped and bleeding, but at least they didn't hurt very much. "Well," I said, "it could have been worse."

"Sure. It could have been a *lot* worse," Garrett said. "You could have been killed! What were you thinking?"

"For your information, I didn't start it. He did. Besides, he didn't look all that strong." I shuffled my feet around in the powdery black dirt. "I thought I could handle him."

"Oh, you handled him all right. Wait till you get a look at your face."

"My face?" Until that very moment, I hadn't even noticed the stinging pain. But once I did, I knew things were pretty bad. Not only did my forehead feel like somebody had slid into home plate on it, but my nose was already swelling, and my right cheek was keeping rhythm with my heart. "Grief," I muttered.

Garrett took my arm, and I limped toward the sidewalk.

CHAPTER · 2

I HOBBLED PAST THE FRONT OF ST. MICHAEL'S CATHOLIC Church. Each step was like walking through a torture chamber, and my throat felt like a ton of dirt had been vacuumed through my mouth. We were only a few yards from the house, when we saw Trooper galloping toward us.

"Don't, Trooper, don't!" Garrett yelled, but it was too late. Before we could stop him, the Belgian shepherd jumped up, plopped his humongous black paws on my shoulders, and started licking my raw face. It felt like sandpaper on a day-old sunburn. "Stop it, Trooper!" Garrett shouted, trying to grab his collar.

"No!" a deep voice echoed from across the street. "Down!"

The retired police dog immediately dropped to a lying position, but his tail still swished back and forth.

Mr. Ed skidded to a stop in front of the dog. He pointed to the ground and said, "Stay!" He removed his green ball cap, revealing a shaved head. "I'm so sorry, Bits—" he started. "What happened to you?"

"It's nothing, really." I stumbled as I tried to walk.

"Here, let me help you," Mr. Ed said. He replaced his cap and reached down, putting one arm behind my knees and the other around my back. My mind cleared through the fog enough to realize he was getting ready to pick me up—like a little baby!

"No!" I yelled, pushing away.

He stepped back, his forehead wrinkled in confusion. "I'm only trying to help you."

"I mean, no, thank you. I can make it." I limped away at a snail's pace, with Garrett on one side and Mr. Ed on the other.

Mr. Ed turned back to Trooper. "Heel!" he commanded. Trooper jumped up, got in place on Mr. Ed's left side, and escorted us down the sidewalk.

By the time we reached the steps to the yellow house, Mrs. Price was scrambling out the front door with Ellie. Her little brother, Nicolas, toddled close behind.

Ellie's mom ran to me and put her arm around my shoulders. "Bitsy! Oh, my goodness, honey, are you okay?"

The truth is, I wasn't okay. And it sure would've felt good to go ahead and cry and get a little sympathy right about then. But I couldn't look like a sissy in front of my friends or Mr. Ed.

"Yes, ma'am, I'm fine." I faked a smile to the cop.

"Thank you for your help." The dog was still in position beside him, wagging his tail. "Don't be mad at Trooper. He didn't know."

Mr. Ed faced Ellie's mom. "Let me know if there's anything I need to do. I may be retired from the police force, but I'm still a cop at heart."

Mrs. Price patted his arm and said, "Thanks, Ed. I'll be in touch." Taking my bloodied hand, she helped me up the steps and through the hallway toward the bathroom.

I rounded the corner . . . and thought I was going to faint. There, in the mirror, was my disgusting face, one brown eye staring back at me.

"Hello, pretty girl. Hello."

I turned my back on my bloody image and faced Mooshew, Garrett's pink cockatoo. Perched on Garrett's yellow head, the talking bird began to dance back and forth from one leg to the other. "Pretty girl, pretty girl," he repeated.

"Yeah, Mooshew, I'm real pretty, aren't I?" I plopped down on the side of the tub.

Nicolas got down on all fours, crawled under Ellie's legs, and smashed into my bloody knees.

"Ow!" I bent over and grabbed my legs.

"Nicolas!" Mrs. Price said.

But before she could nab him, he poked his pointer finger right into my swollen eye. My vision was covered in white-hot light.

"Bitsy boo-boo, Garrett. Bitsy boo-boo, Momm—"

Mrs. Price grabbed the baby and set him in the hall. "Okay, everybody out." She shooed my friends toward the bathroom door.

"But, Mom—" Garrett started.

His mother pointed. "Out. Now."

"Come on, Mooshew." Garrett held his arm out for the bird. "We can tell when we're not wanted."

Mooshew jumped from Garrett's head, and they started out of the bathroom. Ellie elbowed her brother out of the way and started toward me.

"And just where do you think you're going, young lady?" her mother asked.

Ellie stopped in her tracks but didn't look up. "Um, to help Bitsy."

"I said, 'Out.' That means you, too."

"But I'm her best friend," Ellie whined.

Mrs. Price took a deep breath and gave Ellie a half smile. "Yes, you are. But she doesn't need a friend right now. She needs a mother."

Ellie's baby-blue eyes begged, but Mrs. Price nodded toward the hallway and said, "Keep your eye on Nicolas." My best friend shuffled out the door, and her mother closed it.

That's when I finally lost it. Mrs. Price sat on the toilet lid and pulled me onto her lap, bloody mess and all. Then she put her arms around me and stroked my hair while the story tumbled out.

"He . . . he didn't look . . . that strong." I sniffled between the words. "I . . . I thought I could . . . handle him."

She didn't say anything, but pressed her cheek against the top of my head and patted my leg.

"But once he got in my face, I couldn't stop it. I didn't know what to d-do."

Mrs. Price took a slow, deep breath.

Here it comes, I thought. *This is where I get what's coming to me.*

But she sat me up and motioned to the side of the tub. It was really hard to move my legs, and the swelling in my cheek covered part of the vision out of my right eye, but I hobbled over and sat down.

Ellie's mom cleared her throat. "Bitsy, I know you think you're pretty tough—"

"I am," I interrupted. "Well, usually I am."

"But the point is, you don't have to be. Nobody expects you to be as tough as the boys, especially those that are bigger and older than you."

"But *I* expect it."

Mrs. Price sighed. "Look, you're becoming a young lady. Don't you think it's time to start acting like one?"

Now, don't get me wrong here. I know that Mrs. Price was concerned about me, and I really did appreciate it. But she has no idea what it's like to be smaller than everyone else. She has no idea what it's like to have people patting you on the head, telling you how "cute" you are. I don't want to be cute—I want to be taken seriously. And if I can't get it by being tall enough, then I'll get it by being tough enough. It usually works. But it obviously didn't work with Ernie Van Tache.

"I don't want to be a sissy ol' girl."

"Bitsy, you're going to have to face it. You *are* a girl. And like it or not, certain things are expected of you. A fistfight with the neighborhood bully is not one of them."

"But I didn't start it."

"You didn't walk away, either, did you?"

"No, ma'am." I peered at her through my swollen slits. "Are you going to make me go home?"

She laughed. "Go home? Oh, Bitsy, of course not. But I do expect you to use better judgment in the future. If you have a problem with something—or someone—while you're here, just come to me. I can help." Then she smiled and put out her hand. "Deal?"

A pain shot through my shoulder as I raised my dirty, blood-smeared hand up to hers. "Deal."

"Good, now let's get you cleaned up so you can practice for the talent show."

I jumped up from the tub. "The talent show? Oh, no, I forgot all about that!" Every inch of my body screamed in pain as my mouth screamed the words. "I can't be in the talent show now. Look at me!"

"Don't say that. You might look just fine by Saturday. Besides, makeup can do wonders."

Me in makeup? Is she dreaming or something? I plopped back down on the tub. "Uh, I don't think I could do that. I don't think I could wear makeup."

She dismissed the thought with a wave of her hand. "Oh, don't be silly, of course you can."

There was no way in the world they would catch me wearing makeup. But how could I say that to Ellie's mom? "I'm . . . uh . . . I'm just not a makeup kind of girl."

Mrs. Price took in a big breath and sighed the air back out. "Bitsy, do you want to win the talent show?"

"Oh, yes, ma'am. I have to. I need that hundred dollars to go to camp."

"Well, all I can say is, if you plan to win, you'd better plan to wear makeup."

I crossed my arms over my dirty, bloodstained shirt. "Grief!"

CHAPTER · 3

SUPPER THAT NIGHT WAS GREAT. MRS. PRICE HAD FIXED dinner for a family who had a new baby, so it was late by the time we ate. But it was worth the wait. Not only did we have lasagna, my most favorite food in the whole wide world, but Mr. Price had gotten doughnuts for dessert, too. They sure beat the leftover honey buns Daddy brought home from his bread route every day.

And things were good after supper, too. Nobody wanted my mangled, bleeding hands to touch anything, especially anything that had to do with food, so I just sat at the table and supervised the cleanup. I was in the middle of explaining that dishes rinsed in hot water dry faster than those rinsed in cold water when Mooshew let out a bloodcurdling screech. Giant pink wings took over the kitchen as the bird flapped and screeched, flapped and screeched, trying to get out the window.

"Mooshew, stop it!" Garrett ordered. The bird, still squawking, landed on a curtain rod.

Ellie dropped the dirty lasagna pan into the sink and offered her dripping arm. "Here, Mooshew. It's okay."

But Mooshew wasn't okay.

Garrett grabbed a kitchen chair and climbed up, putting himself eye level with the frantic bird. He opened his hand, held out his arm, and spoke softly. "Come on, Mooshew."

Two screeches later, the bird flitted to his welcoming hand. "That's a good boy," Garrett reassured him.

Mooshew's black eyes monitored the window as Garrett placed him back on the tree-like perch. "It's okay, Mooshew, see? Nothing's out there." Garrett leaned toward the window and squinted.

Trooper barked outside.

"What was that?" Garrett whispered, almost to himself.

"It was just Trooper," Ellie said.

"No, not Trooper." He pointed across the backyard. "What's that?"

Ellie ran while I shuffled to the window. We pushed our way around her thirteen-year-old brother just in time to see a flicker of light inside the creepy old house next door.

Mooshew paced back and forth across his perch, like a soldier guarding Buckingham Palace.

"What's so weird about a light?" I said. "Maybe your neighbors just got home."

Another flash peeked through the blinds at the house next door.

Ellie sucked in a quick breath and covered her mouth. "There it is again!"

I rolled my eyes.

Garrett leaned his forehead against the window and squinted his blue eyes once more. "Well, if that's it, we have a ghost for a neighbor. Mr. Hawkins was the only person living there, and he died a few months ago."

"A ghost?" Ellie said, her eyes as big as soccer balls. "Do you think it could really be a ghost?"

I laughed. "Get real. A ghost?"

Garrett headed back to the sink. "Well, standing here arguing about it isn't going to get us anywhere. Come on, let's finish up these dishes." He glanced at me and winked. "Then we can figure out who the ghost is."

After Garrett and Ellie cleaned the kitchen, we hurried up the stairs. Actually, they hurried and I hobbled.

"Where are y'all going in such a rush?" Mrs. Price asked as Garrett and Ellie dashed by the bathroom. Baby Nicolas was splashing in the tub.

Ellie spoke up first. "Oh, we're through with the dishes, so we thought we'd play a game."

"Okay, but be sure you clean up your mess when you're done. We have that open house tomorrow night."

I looked at my friends and mouthed, "Open house?"

They shrugged.

I turned to Ellie's mom. "What's an open house?"

Mrs. Price rinsed the baby's back. "It's sort of a party. It's part of a fund-raiser to turn that empty house next door into a resource center."

"You mean the creepy house?" I asked.

"How are we doing that?" Garrett said. "We don't know anything about fixing up a house, especially one that looks that bad."

Then Ellie put in her two cents worth. "Besides, we don't have any money, remember? At least that's what you said last week when I told you I needed a new leotard. Personally, I don't see how we can afford to fix up that old house when we can't even buy a little ol' leotard."

Their mother peered sideways at Ellie. "Well, first of all, you *wanted* a new leotard, you didn't *need* one. There's a difference. These people need a resource center. People like Ricky."

"You mean the man who works at the grocery store? The one who wears white coveralls?" Ellie asked. She turned to me. "You'd like him. He reminds me of a big kid, especially when he laughs."

"Yes, he's the one," Mrs. Price said. "He's a sweet guy, and he is a lot of fun, but life isn't easy for him. His mother's getting pretty old now, and I don't know how much longer she can take care of him."

I felt bad for that Ricky fellow, but I could think of a lot of things I really needed, too. Like the money to pay bill collectors who came late at night, some decent food at our house, a hundred dollars for camp—

Mrs. Price interrupted my thoughts. "You're right about one thing, though. We can't do it by ourselves. But when a group of people work together, a lot can be accomplished." She squeezed the baby shampoo onto Nicolas's wet hair and started scrubbing.

"So who's going to help fix up the house?" Garrett asked.

"There's a bunch of people, actually. After Mr. Hawkins died and donated the house to the city, your dad and I joined a committee to decide what to do with it. Ed's working on it, too. We all agreed it was best to have an auction and sell the stuff inside the house. So tomorrow evening people will go over there, check out everything, and decide what they want to bid on, then they'll come over here for refreshments."

"Will we have cookies and cake and stuff?" Ellie asked.

"Uh-huh," Mrs. Price answered. "Friday we'll have the auction, and the money we get will be used to fix the house up as a resource center, one that'll offer training for the handicapped—like Ricky—or counseling for troubled kids."

"That's a great idea," I said. Then I snapped my fingers. "Hey, Ernie could be your first patient. He'd make a great experiment!"

Garrett and Ellie laughed, but Mrs. Price didn't say

a word. She tilted her head, raised one eyebrow, and gave me "the look." She said, "They're called 'clients,' not 'patients,' and nobody's experimenting on anyone. The center will help with job placement for disabled adults and therapy for foster kids."

"Like I said, a place for Ernie."

Mrs. Price went to the bathroom closet and pulled out a Buzz Lightyear towel.

"So that explains the light in Mr. Hawkins's house," Ellie said.

"What light?" her mother asked.

Garrett leaned against the doorframe. "We saw something over there while we were cleaning up the kitchen. A light or something. Guess someone was just working on the auction."

Mrs. Price walked across the room. "Hmm, not that I know of. We have the only key." She looked out the window and down toward the empty house. "I don't see a light now. Maybe it was a reflection from a car or something." She walked back to the tub, placed the towel on the floor, and knelt down. "I'm so excited about this auction," she said, pouring a cup of water over Nicolas's head. "It's such a worthwhile project."

Garrett joined his mother and put his arm around her shoulders. "You're right, Mom, it is a good project. Can I help?"

Ellie joined them, leaned forward against her mom's back, and hugged her. "Me, too?"

There was a moment of silence as everyone waited for me to make a move. Nicolas asked, "Bitsy hug Mommy, too?"

I laughed and limped over to the tangled family. Taking the spot opposite Garrett, I placed my arm over his. "Got room for one more?"

Nicolas threw a cup of bathwater in the air, then clapped his hands in rhythm. "Bitsy hug Mommy! Bitsy hug Mommy!"

It was a really touching moment, like those Hallmark card commercials. You know, the kind that makes you cry, even when it's happy. But underneath the noise of the clapping and the laughing and the squealing was a scratchy, faraway screech, like Mooshew was sending a warning from his perch below.

CHAPTER · 4

THE NEXT MORNING I WOKE UP EARLY AND LIMPED TO the mirror in Ellie's room. It was worse than I'd thought. My swollen face made me look like a bruised, battered pig with a slit where my right eye should be. I checked out the rest of the damage. It didn't look good.

How in the world was I supposed to sing about being a prissy girl when I looked like this? I knew it wasn't a good idea from the moment Mother first suggested it back home.

"Just think, Bitsy," she'd said. "Nobody else will be singing anything like 'I Enjoy Being a Girl.' You can dress up in a frilly dress and wear pearls and dance and really turn on the charm. And the fact that you're a pretty girl doesn't hurt, either."

"But Mother, I'm not prissy, I'm a tomboy. And the truth is, I don't enjoy being a *girl.* I enjoy being a *kid.*" I folded my arms. "I'd be lying if I sang that song." Mother was a stickler when it came to lying.

She smiled and shook her head. "Nice try, but it's not a lie when it's only a song in a talent show." Then she put her hand on my shoulder. "Look, it's your contest, and I'm not going to tell you what to do. But I am telling you this: singing 'I Enjoy Being a Girl' is your best chance at winning the talent show. And winning the talent show is your only chance of having the money for camp."

Mother was right about one thing, winning Amelia Island's July Fourth Talent Show was my only hope as far as camp was concerned. Money didn't grow on trees back in Greenville, South Carolina, and it certainly didn't grow on any trees in our little yard. We did good to have money for food; money for camp was out of the question. I needed a plan to get well as soon as possible. I needed a plan to look good.

I limped back to Ellie's bed. "Wake up," I said, pulling back the covers. "We've got some planning to do."

We sat cross-legged on Ellie's bed, my collection of jewelry spread out before us. I picked up a gold chain with the letter "E" hanging from it. "Here," I said, "put this on."

"I don't have the money to buy any of your jewelry," Ellie said. "I told you that already."

"Don't worry about it."

She lifted her blonde hair so I could hook the clasp.

Then she turned around to face me. "I don't understand. How are you going to make any money for camp if you give away all your Bitsy's Bangles?"

"I'm not giving it all away. I'm just giving you one little necklace. It's called good advertising. Daddy taught me all about it. And he should know, with all the businesses he's had. See, you wear the necklace everywhere you go. Your friends will see it and they'll want one. I'm the only one who has them, so they'll come, see my entire collection of Bitsy's Bangles, and spend gobs of money. I'll have that hundred dollars in no time."

"Oh," Ellie said. "Guess I never thought about it that way."

"That's 'cause you're not in business for yourself. All us business people look at things differently. It's part of our makeup."

Ellie's eyebrows scrunched up. "I thought you said you weren't going to wear any makeup."

I rubbed my forehead and shook my head. "That's not what I'm talking about, Ellie. I mean—"

"Kids, it's time for breakfast now," Mrs. Price yelled from downstairs.

"I'll explain later," I said. "Let's get down there and tell your mom about our plans before she fixes something I can't eat."

Ellie took off, leaving me there alone to pack up my jewelry. I gathered the cards of gold pierced earrings and stacked them in the shoe box. Then I picked up the necklaces, carefully separating the initials and putting them in alphabetical order, the way Daddy showed me.

Not many kids my age have their own business. But not many kids have a daddy like mine. One day we'll strike it rich together, and then we'll have nice clothes and lots of food in the cupboard, and the mailbox will be full of money instead of past-due bills. One day Daddy's dreams will come true, and so will mine.

And then the idea hit me—the best advertising promotion I could ever dream of! I put my business shoe box back into the closet and limped down to share the news.

Nicolas banged his sippy cup on the high chair. "Pop-Tart! Pop-Tart! Pop-Tart!" he yelled in rhythm to his cup.

Mrs. Price squeezed her lips as she walked over to him and stood perfectly still. She didn't say a word. The baby took one look at his mother and stopped banging. He smiled, his white teeth shining. "Pop-Tart."

"Excuse me?" his mother said.

"Um . . . Pop-Tart . . . pwease?"

"That's better." Then she turned to me. "Bitsy, Ellie tells me you don't want a Pop-Tart for breakfast this morning. What's up? Are you feeling okay?"

I struggled into my chair. "Yes, ma'am, I'm feeling much better. I just figured I'd eat healthy for a few days.

You know, cut out the sugar and fat. Maybe it'll help my face get well faster."

"You know I'm all for eating healthy," Mrs. Price said, "but are you sure you want to cut out all of your sugar and fat? Isn't that kind of drastic?"

I threw my shoulders back and sat up straight. I looked at her with my left eye, my right eye trying to peek through the tiny opening. "Drastic results take drastic measures, don't you think?"

"I guess. So what do you want instead?"

"How about a hard-boiled egg, wheat toast with no butter or jelly, and a glass of milk? Oh, and do you have any vitamins? That might help, too."

"She can have one of mine," Garrett offered. He jumped up from the table and grabbed the bottle from the counter. "You want Fred or Wilma?"

I picked an orange Wilma and popped it into my mouth. It tasted pretty good. I felt stronger already.

It was time for my announcement. I stood and cleared my throat. "Could I have everyone's attention please? I have a new promotion for Bitsy's Bangles, and I want my friends to be the first to know."

Everyone stopped what they were doing and gathered around the table, even Ellie's mom. Everyone, that is, except Nicolas, who continued to slurp and chomp his way through breakfast.

"I want you all to know that I've come up with the best advertising promotion ever."

"Huh?" Ellie said. My best friend was in the dark when it came to business.

"What is it?" Garrett asked.

Mrs. Price leaned against the counter, wiping her hands on a damp towel.

I put on a big smile. "You, my friends, are the first to know that beginning today, I'm offering a double-your-money-back guarantee on all Bitsy's Bangles."

Ellie stared at me, as if she hadn't even heard the incredible announcement. Garrett went back to eating his breakfast. Nicolas banged his sippy cup.

Mrs. Price pulled out a chair and sat down. "Double your money back? Are you sure you want to do that?"

"Of course. Why not? More people would buy my jewelry, and that would mean more money in my camp fund. Sounds like a perfect plan to me."

"But you could lose money. You could go in the hole."

"How can I lose money if I'm selling more jewelry?"

"Bitsy, if you offer double money back, you have to be prepared to honor it. If someone pays five dollars for a necklace, you'd have to give them ten dollars if they return it for some reason."

I placed my hand on Mrs. Price's shoulder. It was obvious *she* didn't understand business either. "That's why I have restrictions on the guarantee. People can't just say they don't like it. There has to be a real reason for them to get their money back."

She brushed the hair back from her face. "But what if there is a real reason?"

"What kind of reason could there possibly be? It's great jewelry at a great price. And that is a great deal."

Garrett's mother took my hand in hers. "Just remember this conversation, Bitsy. Remember that you're making a promise to people that you have to keep, regardless of what it may mean to your business."

"Don't worry, I know what I'm doing. This is going to mean lots of business for Bitsy's Bangles. Just wait and see. This is going to be big. Really big."

Mrs. Price poked her head into the bathroom. "Hurry up, girls. We're leaving for the beach in ten minutes, whether you're ready or not."

Ellie picked up a bottle and sprayed her straw-colored hair.

"What's that?" I asked.

"Sun-Glow. It makes your hair blonder. You just spray it on and go out in the sun. The stuff does all the work. All my friends are using it."

"All your friends except me," I said, talking to her reflection in the mirror. "Grief."

Ellie turned from the mirror and faced me. "It's just—"

"What? It's just what?"

"It's just everybody I know who's using it has blonde hair."

"So? Does brown hair make me a second-class citizen?"

"No. It's—"

"Hey, you know what? I hate to admit it, but this might be one time that blonde is better."

"What?"

"Think about it, Ellie. Girls who really enjoy being girls are usually blonde, right? They're the girly-girls, the priss-pots."

Ellie glared at me.

"All except you, of course. You're not like most blondes I know. But you do have to admit, you're prissier than me."

"Bitsy, every girl I know is prissier than you."

I rubbed my bruised chin and ignored her smart-aleck comment. "Yeah, it might actually be good to be blonde this one time." I turned to Ellie. "It'll go away, won't it? I like being brunette."

"I don't really know too much about it. Mom just said I could use it if I wanted to, so I am."

"Then she won't mind if I use it, too. Oh man, this is going to be great! Good food and vitamins to get me well, and blonde hair, too. This talent show is going to be a piece of cake!"

CHAPTER · 5

MRS. PRICE HELD NICOLAS ON HER HIP AS SHE OPENED the back door and we pushed our way through. "Do y'all have your towels and beach toys?"

"Got mine," Garrett said.

"Me, too," Ellie and I said together.

Their mother flipped the lock and grabbed the doorknob. "Be a good boy, Mooshew," she said as she shut the door.

He flapped his wings and gazed out the window. We filed out the door, and Mooshew watched us pile into the red van.

Mrs. Price backed out of the driveway and started up the road. "Oh, look," she said, pointing to the creepy house. "The sign is up about the open house this evening and the auction Friday at four."

"I sure miss Mr. Hawkins," Ellie said from the back.

"I don't," Garrett said. "He was mean. But I do miss his lemon drops."

Their mother eyed us through the rearview mirror. "He was gruff, all right, but he was still kind at heart. Remember that time he gave y'all those old baseball cards and that antique Barbie doll? He didn't have to do that. I think he wanted to be nice but just didn't know how. He never was around people very much."

"Yeah, I can see why people didn't want to be around him," Garrett said.

"He didn't really have any relatives," Mrs. Price said, "except his nephew—you know, Shorty Owens, the man who owns Shorty's grocery store."

"That's where Ricky works, isn't it?" Ellie asked.

"Sure is," her mother answered.

"Well," Garrett said, "I guess Mr. Shorty will get a lot of his family's stuff from the house."

"No, I'm afraid not," Mrs. Price answered. "There's been some old family feud, and they haven't spoken to each other in years. Shorty can't even bid on anything in the house—it says so in Mr. Hawkins's will."

"I told you he was mean," Garrett said. Then he pointed to the sidewalk. "Uh-oh. Isn't that Ernie and Bernie?"

I caught Ellie's reflection as she stuck her tongue out at the twins.

"Don't be a sissy," I whispered.

"Now, kids, don't worry about them or what they're doing," Mrs. Price said. "Just stay out of their way, and you'll be fine. Bitsy, that means you, too."

"You don't have to worry about me. I'm staying as far away from those twins as I can."

We reached Main Beach and climbed out of the van. "Don't forget your sunscreen," Mrs. Price yelled as we took off for the sand and water.

"What a neat place!" I said. "Y'all are so lucky. This is like living on Tybee Island."

"Oh, boy, here we go again," Garrett said, plopping down on his towel and grabbing the sunscreen.

"Very funny. For your information, I was just going to point out that Amelia has a lighthouse and fort ruins and Blackbeard, just like at Tybee Island." Then I snickered. "I hope things go better here than they did there."

"You're certainly off to a great start with Ernie," Garrett said.

I gave a half smile to my friend and hobbled off toward the water. The three of us rode the waves for a while, then Ellie and I decided to bury Garrett in the sand.

"Why does it have to be me?" he asked, trying to sound disappointed.

"Because girls always bury guys, that's why," Ellie said.

Even though it hurt my knees, I knelt down and started digging in the wet sand. "Just be a good sport and help us get the hole ready. I'll try not to think about what I dug up at Tybee."

Garrett and Ellie joined me on the ground. "Yeah,

maybe we'll be the ones to find a skeleton this time!" Garrett said.

"You wish," I said.

We were hard at work when Mrs. Price walked up. "I've got to take Nicolas to the restroom to clean him up. Will you guys be okay for a few minutes?"

"Sure, mom," Ellie answered. "We're not babies, you know."

"I know, but I still don't want you getting in the water until I get back."

"We won't," we promised.

"We're having too much fun!" Ellie added.

Their mom headed toward the restroom, Nicolas dragging his feet in the sand.

"Okay, try it, Garrett," I said.

He jumped in and stretched out. "Yep, just right. Now y'all cover me up."

"With pleasure," I answered. Ellie and I quickly covered Garrett with loose sand and then began to pack it into a hard mass. "Come on, Ellie, let's make a big mound."

"Thanks a lot," Garrett said, laughing. "I can't move now as it is!"

We packed bucket after bucket of sand on top of the mound and smoothed it into a hard, oval grave.

"Look at the little babies having fun in the sand," a voice called behind us.

We twisted around and shielded the sun from our

eyes. It was Ernie! And he looked as bad as I did. Scratch for scratch and bruise for bruise, I'd say we had a tie.

Bernie yawned and covered her mouth. "Ernie, don't start anything." Then she smiled.

Ernie winked as he smiled back. "You know I'd never do that, sis. I never start anything. But I do finish it!" At that instant he pulled back his scraped left leg and kicked a load of sand right into Garrett's face.

Then he spun around and took off. Garrett coughed, trying to get his breath. Before I knew what I was doing, I caught up to Ernie and stood eyeball-to-eyeball with the bully.

"What do you think you're doing?" I screamed.

"Aw, nothing. Just showing the chicken who's boss."

"Oh, you're real brave, all right." I sneered. "It takes a lot of guts to kick sand at someone who's buried, someone who can't fight back."

"You know, you might just have a point there, Betsy Wetsy. Sorry about that. I guess I should have been fighting with *you*!" With that, he threw me to the sand, dropped down, and rubbed my face in the dry powder.

I fought and kicked and scratched until I got his hands off my head. He took off running. I sputtered and spit, trying not to breathe in the sand, wiping the grit out of my eyes.

"Bitsy, hurry!" Ellie yelled. "The tide's coming in. We've got to get Garrett out!"

I stumbled my way back to the hard, packed mound and clawed at the sand as fast as I could. The waves splashed across the bottom of the sand heap.

"Hurry!" Garrett yelled. "Get me out!"

Another wave of salty water rolled halfway up the length of Garrett's body. "You've got to help us," I yelled at him. "Move your arms and legs inside."

"What do you think I'm doing—taking a nap? I *am* trying to get out!"

A layer of foam rolled up and stopped at Garrett's chin. His foot poked through at the bottom of the mound.

"Keep wiggling, don't stop!" I yelled.

Ellie moved to Garrett's feet and dug faster. His legs broke free just as another ocean wave splashed over him, covering his mouth. He spit and took in a deep breath.

I looked up to see the biggest wave yet, heading right toward us. "Dig, Ellie! Help us, Garrett!" I clawed deeper into the sand and felt his shoulder. "Move, Garrett, move!" I found his arm and pulled.

The wave raced across his feet as I jerked his arm with all my might. Garrett broke through the mound of sand and sat up just as the water covered his open grave.

Ellie and I dropped to the wet ground.

"Well," Garrett said between gasps of breath, "does this beat the Tybee Island skeleton?"

CHAPTER · 6

MRS. PRICE WAS NOT HAPPY. "HOW COULD THOSE TWINS do such a thing? Just wait till I tell their aunt about this. They obviously have more problems than I thought."

We all just sat in the back of the van, keeping our mouths closed, afraid to say a word.

But their mother wasn't finished. "Maybe I should talk to Mr. Ed. He knows about police stuff. Kids like that don't even deserve to be out on the street. They need to be locked up in juvenile hall." The tires squealed as she turned the van into the driveway.

"Does this mean the house next door won't be a resource center after all?" Ellie asked.

Garrett and I gave her a dirty look.

"What?" she whispered.

Mrs. Price drove behind the yellow house, stopped the car, and put it in park. She turned around in her seat and faced the back. "What do you mean? What does that have to do with anything?"

"Well, you said yesterday the resource center would be for foster kids. If foster kids are going to be locked up, then we won't need a center, right?"

Garrett glared at his sister.

Their mother took in a deep breath, tightened her lips, and faced the front. Then, without saying a word, she got out of the van, unbuckled Nicolas's car seat, and carried him into the house.

"Thanks a lot, Ellie," Garrett said after his mother had left the van.

"What? What'd I do?"

"Oh, nothing much. You just got Mom into the worst mood ever."

"I don't know," I said. "I think she was sad, not mad."

"What would she have to be sad about?" Garrett asked.

"I'm not sure, but—" I began. "Shush! Here she comes."

Mrs. Price stuck her head through the open side door. "Come on in, kids. We need to talk." Without another word, she spun around and walked back toward the house.

Garrett unbuckled his seat belt and climbed over his sister. "Like I said, thanks a lot."

We grabbed our stuff, jumped from the van, and headed to the back door.

Mooshew was sitting on his perch. "Hello, pretty girl. Pretty girl," he said.

"Hello," I answered.

"How do you know he was talking to you?" Garrett said as we tromped into the kitchen. "He calls everybody a pretty girl, even me."

"Hey, don't jump all over me just 'cause you're mad at your sister. Take it out on her."

Mrs. Price walked into the kitchen and pulled out a chair. "Nobody's taking anything out on anyone, including me. Have a seat."

We gathered around the table and sat down. No one spoke. After a moment, Mrs. Price cleared her throat.

Here it comes, I thought.

"First," she said, "I want to apologize."

We all watched each other but kept our mouths shut.

"I want to apologize for talking bad about Ernie."

"You don't need to apologize, Mrs. Price." The words came out before I knew what I was doing. "If anybody deserves to be talked bad about, it's Ernie." I patted her arm to show my sincerity.

She put her hand over mine and said, "See, that's exactly what I mean. I shouldn't have talked about him that way. I set a bad example for you . . . for all of you."

Garrett tried to reason with his mother. "But Mom, you know what he did to us. I think juvenile hall is exactly what he needs."

"Son, it's easy for me and you and Ellie and Bitsy to sit here and judge Ernie. We've had an easy life. We've had everything we need."

I wasn't sure that now was the best time to point it out, but I wouldn't exactly call my life an easy one. It's hard sharing a room with three other kids. And I sure don't have everything I need. What about the money for camp . . . and some decent food?

"And most of all," she went on, "you have parents who love you, who'd give their lives for you."

She had me on that one. Sure, sometimes it was hard living the way we live, with our little house and no money for extras. But there's one thing I've always known—my parents love me. They would die for me.

She continued. "What have Ernie and Bernie had? A life without parents, and an aunt who has to work all the time. Can you imagine being thirteen and not having a mother?" Mrs. Price reached across the table, grabbed a napkin, and caught a tear just before it fell from her cheek. "They need friends. They need us."

This wasn't sounding good. "Us?" I said.

"But, Mom," Garrett said, "what can we possibly do?"

"We could be their friends," she replied.

"But how can we be friends with people who are always beating us up?" Ellie asked.

"Hey, he didn't beat me up," I corrected. "It was a tie."

"We can all help them by being nice," Mrs. Price said, "even if it is at a distance."

"I agree," I said.

Garrett and Ellie questioned me with their eyes.

"I agree they need help from somebody. Anybody!" I giggled, and my friends joined in.

Mrs. Price didn't crack a smile. "They do need help, and we're going to be the ones to give it. I'll call Myrna and let her know what happened, and then I'll invite the kids to go to church with you for choir practice this afternoon."

We quit laughing. "What?" I asked.

"Tell me you're not serious," Ellie begged.

Mrs. Price nodded her head.

Garrett tried to talk some sense into his mother. "But Ernie will do something awful, like pound our heads in beat to the music. Please, Mom, don't make us do that. Anything but that!"

She sat quietly for a moment. "Maybe that *is* asking for too much too fast. But promise me one thing. Promise me you'll ask God to show you how to be friends with Ernie and Bernie."

What could we say? We had to agree, or else we'd find our heads on the losing end of "Amazing Grace."

We all said we'd pray for them, and us. My prayer was simple: "God, please help us stay out of Ernie's way."

CHAPTER 7

ELLIE AND I SPENT THE NEXT HOUR CALLING ALL HER friends and telling them about my wonderful jewelry. They were really excited when they heard I'd personally bring my portable store to choir practice later that afternoon. Things were really going good.

After the sales calls, I went to the bathroom and added more Sun-Glow. Then I headed to the kitchen for another glass of milk.

We were about to leave for choir practice when the phone rang.

Mrs. Price answered it. "Hi, Ruth. So good to hear from you."

My mother! I held my breath, waiting to see if Mrs. Price was going to report on my little problem with Ernie.

"We're having a great time with Bitsy. She's always such a joy to be around."

I breathed a sigh of relief. Mrs. Price listened and

then laughed. My mom must have said something funny. I hoped it wasn't about me.

"Okay," Mrs. Price said, "here she is." She handed me the phone.

"Mother?" I said into the receiver. "Is everything okay?"

"Of course it is. Why?" my mother asked.

"Well, I know long-distance calls cost a lot of money, so I figured something must be wrong for you to call me."

Mother laughed. "Nothing's wrong, but I do need to talk to you."

My heart bounced in my chest like a Ping-Pong ball.

"I wanted to let you know you got a letter today from WYFF, Channel Four," she said. "Do you know what that would be about?"

"From WYFF? Are you serious?"

"Of course I'm serious. Were you expecting something from them?"

"I'm not sure I really expected to hear anything, but I did write them a letter."

"A letter? About what?"

"Well . . . I kind of asked them if I could be on TV."

Ellie's eyes danced. Garrett just smiled.

"You what?" Mother asked.

"What did they say? Can I be on TV?"

"I don't know. I didn't open the letter."

"You didn't open it? Why not?"

"Because it's not addressed to me, silly. Do you want me to open it now?"

"Yes! Yes, please!" I could hear the envelope ripping apart as my mother pulled out the letter. "Hurry! What does it say?"

"Just a minute. I'm getting it. Okay, it says: 'Dear Bitsy, Thank you for your interesting letter. What a treat to hear from someone as talented as you. I would appreciate the opportunity to meet with you and one of your parents this week. Please contact our office at 555-0413 to schedule an appointment as soon as possible. Sincerely, Norvin Duncan, Station Manager.'"

I jumped up and down and grabbed Ellie's shoulder. "He wants to meet me! He really wants to meet me!"

Ellie jumped up and down too.

"Maybe I'll have my own TV show," I said.

"Whoa, wait a minute," my mother said. "He just wants to meet you—that's all we know."

"Yes, but why would he want to meet me as soon as possible if he didn't have plans for me?"

"I know it's hard, Bitsy, but let's take this one step at a time. What do you want me to do about the letter?"

"Would you call him? Would you call him and explain that I'm out of town and I'll be home next week? You or Daddy could go next week, couldn't you?"

"Of course we could. Don't worry, I'll take care of it as soon as we hang up the phone."

"Can you call me back and let me know what he says? Please?"

"No. You know I can't pay for another phone call."

"But Mother—"

"You heard me."

Then I remembered my face. "Oh, uh, you might want to make the appointment for Thursday or Friday next week."

"Why?" she asked. "I thought you were anxious to talk to Mr. Duncan."

"Oh, I am! It's just that I had a little . . . a little accident, and it'd be better if my face was healed up before I meet him."

"An accident? What kind of accident? And what's wrong with your face?"

"It's not that bad—" I started.

"Just tell me what happened."

"Well, see, there was this bully, and—"

"A bully? Bitsy, what were you doing with a bully?"

"He started it."

"But what about the decision you made to live at peace with everyone?"

"I know, I know. But Ernie doesn't want to live at peace with anyone. Especially me."

"Bitsy, when are you going to learn?"

"I've learned, Mother. I'm staying away from Ernie and his sister. Now, will you try to make the appointment for later in the week? I'll be fine by then."

"Okay. But Bitsy. . . ."

"Yes, ma'am?"

"Please behave."

"I will. Oh, Mother, aren't you going to wish me luck on the talent show?"

"No, I'm not going to wish you luck, sweetheart, but I promise to pray for you."

It was hard to concentrate on dressing for choir practice. I was finally going to be on TV, and I was about to have the biggest sales day of my business career. All of Ellie's friends wanted their own Bitsy's Bangles, and I was ready. The shoe box was in my backpack, full of necklaces and earrings, every one symbolizing my success as a businesswoman. And, on top of that, I felt lots better. Eating right and taking vitamins was already paying off.

We started down the sidewalk and headed toward the church. But after only a few steps, we realized our path would lead us in front of the twins' house.

"Wait. Let's cut through Mr. Hawkins's backyard," Garrett suggested. "That way we can avoid another confrontation with the demon duo."

Ellie and I liked that idea. We rounded the corner of the creepy house and immediately jumped back into the shadows. There was Ernie, standing outside a broken window, taking a big cardboard box from someone inside. Once he had it securely in his hands, he watched as Bernie climbed out the window and joined him. Then they took off around the far side of the house.

"That explains the light flickering in the house last night," I said.

Ellie nodded.

"Guess so," Garrett said. "But what could the twins possibly want from that old house?"

"Who knows? Who cares?" I said. "At least they're bothering something else instead of us. I say let's be grateful for the little things."

"To the little things!" Garrett said as he started across the backyard.

Ellie and I smiled, hooked arms, and headed toward the church. "To the little things!" we repeated.

CHAPTER · 8

AS SOON AS WE GOT TO CHURCH, ELLIE INTRODUCED me to her friends and explained my injuries. The girls watched me out of the corners of their eyes, but nobody asked any questions. Break time came, and we took over the girls' bathroom.

I set up my own personal office on the plaid sofa. "These," I said, reaching for the gold initial necklaces, "are my most popular design." I pointed to my own gold "B" hanging from my neck. "See how it glitters in the light?"

"I still don't understand why you would fight with Ernie," one of the girls said. "He's the meanest kid in town."

"I told you already that I didn't start it. Now, see these initials—"

"But nobody ever fights Ernie. Not even the boys," someone else added.

"Like I said, I didn't want to fight. He made me."

A girl with blonde curls plopped down on the couch beside me. "Made you? Why didn't you just run away? That's what I would have done."

"Yeah, me too," someone said.

That did it! I wasn't there to talk about Ernie; I was there to sell Bitsy's Bangles. I turned to the yellow-headed scaredy-cat and gave her the evil eye. "Well, I guess that's the difference between you and me. I don't run." I faced the group. "Now, who wants to see this exquisite jewelry?"

Ellie jumped to my rescue. "Listen, everybody, Bitsy's had a terrible experience. I mean, look at her—she almost died in a fight that wasn't even her fault."

"It was a tie," I said, staring at Ellie with my good eye.

She continued like she didn't even hear me. "Why don't we forget about Ernie for a while and look at these necklaces?" She twisted her own "E" and said, "See the sparkle?"

"How much are they?" one of the girls asked.

"Well, they're normally eight dollars," I replied, "but because you're Ellie's friends, I'll sell them to you for only five dollars."

"Five dollars? That's a lot of money," someone said.

"I agree," I said. "It is a lot of money. That's why I make it easy for you by offering a double-your-money-back guarantee. If, for any reasonable reason, you're unhappy with your purchase, I will return not only the five dollars you paid, but give you an extra five dollars as well, for a total of ten dollars."

"You will? Okay, I'll take one. I'd like a 'D' please. For Darcy."

"My name's Mallory. Do you have an 'M' necklace?"

"Do you have a 'C' for Cassie?"

"Whoa, wait a minute," I said. "Everyone will get a chance. My assistant, Ellie, can help you, too."

It took our entire break time, but we did it. The bathroom was empty. Ellie and I sat on the sofa as I counted the money. "Thirty, thirty-five, forty." I tossed the last five-dollar bill onto the stack and said, "We made forty dollars, Ellie. I'm almost halfway to camp already!

"But what did you pay for the necklaces?" Ellie asked. "Don't you have to take that money out for expenses?"

"Oh. Oh, yeah. You're right. They cost me a dollar apiece—that's eight dollars. Forty dollars subtract eight dollars is thirty-two. I still have thirty-two dollars! Where else could a twelve-year-old make thirty-two dollars in less than fifteen minutes? Nowhere, that's where!"

Ellie stood up. "We'd better get back to the group."

"Go ahead. I'll get my things and be there in a minute."

"Okay." She walked out the door.

I collected the scattered necklaces and began putting

them back in alphabetical order. Thirty-two dollars. Why didn't it feel as good as I thought it would? I gathered my things and headed to the rest of the group. Time to get back to choir practice.

It was late afternoon by the time Garrett, Ellie, and I ambled back toward their yellow house. I was still excited about my business. "Thirty-two dollars! Can you believe it, Garrett? Have you ever made thirty-two dollars in fifteen minutes?"

"No, Bitsy, I haven't." He stopped walking and faced me. "Look, I'm happy for you and all, but enough's enough already. Can't we talk about something else, please?"

I opened my mouth to speak but stopped before I could mutter a sound. Pointing behind Garrett toward the twins' house, I said, "How would you like to talk about that?"

Garrett and Ellie followed my finger. There, on the twins' front porch, was Ernie, trying to free his head from between the wrought-iron rails. It wouldn't budge. Garrett, Ellie, and I started laughing at the same time. I bent over and laughed until my stomach hurt.

Bernie stood above her brother and glared at us, her hands on her hips. "Stop it!" she demanded. "Stop it right now!"

"What's the matter with you, scarface?" Ernie yelled from his kneeling position. "Oh, you're real brave when someone can't reach you, aren't you? What's the matter? You afraid to come up here?"

"Not afraid, just smart," I answered between laughs. "Besides, I know how to get your head out."

"You do not!"

"Do, too. It happened to my sister last year, and I had to get her out. How'd you get your head stuck, anyway?"

Bernie started pacing. "It's all my fault. I called him a chicken and dared him to do it. And now he's stuck forever."

"That doesn't make it your fault, Bernie," Garrett said. "Ernie makes his own decisions. But, like a lot of his decisions, this one wasn't very smart."

"Hey, you quit talking about me like I'm not here!" Ernie called from his wrought-iron prison. He tried to pull his head out of the bars again. "You'll be sorry when I get out of here."

I laughed again. "So, when exactly will that be, Ernie? Anytime this year?"

Bernie answered for her brother. "He has to get out now! Aunt Myrna will be here any minute, and she's going to be so mad that we're outside." Looking at Garrett and Ellie, she said, "We've been grounded inside ever since your tattletale mother made that little phone call."

I walked up the pathway to the foot of the steps. "And whose fault was it that she had to make that call?

Has it ever occurred to you that these problems are your own fault?"

Ernie spoke from his position on the floor of the porch. "My fault? Can I help it that y'all are a bunch of wimps?"

Bernie kicked her brother's leg. "Ernie, cut it out. We've got to get you out of there!" Then she looked at me. "Do you really know how to get him out, honest?"

"Sure do." I turned and headed back toward the sidewalk.

"Wait," Ernie called. "Please, wait."

In my heart of hearts, I really wanted to keep walking away. But then I remembered Mrs. Price's lecture and my promise to live at peace with everyone. Maybe Ernie did need a friend. Maybe I could make a difference in his life. Against my better judgment, I turned back to face him. "What do you want?"

"I . . . I could use a little help here."

"I see that, but I need something, too."

"Something from me? What?"

I patted my foot. "I need some honest answers."

Bernie interrupted our little conversation. "Can you two hurry it up? Aunt Myrna will be home any minute."

"Be quiet, Bernie," Ernie said. "What do you want, Bitsy?"

"The truth. First of all, were you two in Mr. Hawkins's house last night? And second of all, did you take a box of stuff from there this afternoon?"

"Are you crazy?" Ernie yelled.

"Just like I thought." I spun around on my heel and headed back toward the Prices' house.

"Wait a minute!" the sister shouted. "Tell her the truth, Ernie. We've got to get you out."

I stopped but kept my back to the twins.

"Okay," Ernie said. "We took the box from the house, but we weren't in there last night."

I started walking away again.

"Really, it's true!" Ernie shouted. Then he almost cried. "Please believe me."

I kept walking.

"Okay, okay. We did it," he said. "We took a box of stuff today and . . . and we were at the house last night."

I turned around in time to see Bernie glaring at her brother with raised eyebrows. "We were not, Ernie!" she shouted, her hands propped on her hips.

I decided to deal with her later. "Go get me some butter and mayonnaise—lots of it!" I hollered as I ran to the porch.

Bernie dashed into the house and was back out in seconds. "Please hurry," she begged as she handed me the supplies.

I reached my hand into the bowl of greasy spread and slapped a handful on Ernie's back.

"Are you crazy?" he yelled. "What are you doing?"

I stopped. "Do you want me to get you out?"

"Yes, of course."

"Then be quiet and do as I say." I continued to rub the butter over his back, and added a glob to his chest and arms. Then I covered his face and spiked head, and added the mayonnaise for good measure. *Might as well make it as humiliating as possible,* I thought.

"Yuck! That's enough!" he said. He tried to pull his head back through the bars. "It still won't work! It still won't work! You lied, you little—"

"No," I answered calmly. "Again, the problem is your own fault. You haven't waited to hear my instructions." I paused for a moment. "Are you ready to listen now?"

"Yes! Hurry up! What do I do?"

"Just squeeze forward through the bars."

"What?"

"Just do it. Turn your body sideways, start with your shoulder, and squeeze yourself forward through the bars."

Bernie dropped to her knees and pushed her brother. "Go, Ernie, go!"

Ernie squinted at me and clenched his teeth, the melting butter and sloppy mayonnaise dripping down his battered face. "This better work." He rotated around and tried to force his body between the rails. His sister pushed. "Ouch!" he yelled, glaring at me.

"It might be painful," I said, "but it's the only way out. Do you want me to help?"

He sighed. "Sure."

I circled around the outside of the porch and

grabbed his right arm. I pulled, Bernie pushed, and Ernie tried to squeeze through.

"Your aunt's coming down the road!" Garrett shouted.

"Yeow!" Ernie yelled as he scraped through the bars and fell to the ground.

I wiped my greasy hands on my shorts and waited for his heartfelt thanks. Instead, he jumped up and shouted, "Get out of here, Betsy Wetsy." Then he added, "Wait, just so you know—we weren't in the house last night. Must have been a ghost." With that, he dashed through the front door.

I joined Garrett and Ellie on the sidewalk seconds before Aunt Myrna pulled into the driveway. She lifted her hand in a halfhearted wave and offered a half smile. We shook our heads and crossed the street to the yellow house.

"Do you think he was telling the truth?" Ellie asked.

"Sure he was," I answered. "The question is, which time?"

CHAPTER · 9

THE DINING ROOM TABLE WAS FULL OF GOODIES I'D promised myself I wouldn't eat. Chocolate chip cookies, brownies, and cheesecake were scattered between the veggie plates and fruit bowl. It was going to be hard to stick to my plan during the open house, but I reminded myself why I needed to eat right this week—I needed to win the talent show. *Life is always about money, isn't it?*

I placed the silverware in a pattern with the napkins, then reached for the china plates.

Ellie dashed in the front door, threw the mail on the dining room table, and headed for the kitchen. "Uh, Mom, Ms. Myrna's at the door. Says she needs to talk to you, right now." Ellie cut her eyes at me and then at Garrett. "She looks mad."

Mrs. Price placed Nicolas in the playpen and walked down the hallway. The rest of us were at the front door before she arrived.

"Hello, Myrna," Mrs. Price said. "What can I do for you?"

"Well, it's really what Ernest and his sister are going to do for you."

I glanced at Garrett and mouthed the question, "Ernest?"

He grinned and covered a laugh.

Ms. Myrna continued. "Looks like the twins have been up to no good again and stole a box of stuff from old Mr. Hawkins's house." She glanced back over her shoulder and looked at Ernie and Bernie sitting on her front porch steps. Then she turned back to us. "I've decided they need punishment for taking the box and for what they did to your kids."

"I tend to agree, Myrna," Ellie's mom answered.

"Good. I'm glad you see it my way. The twins will be over after supper to help wash dishes at the open house."

Mrs. Price stared at the twins' aunt. "Uh, excuse me?"

"Since they beat up your kids and—"

"Ernie didn't beat me up," I said, forcing my way to the front. "It was a tie."

Ms. Myrna looked down her nose and dismissed me like I was a gnat. "As I was saying, since they beat up your kids and stole from the house you're working on, I figured they owed you."

Mrs. Price said, "Thank you for your consideration, Myrna, but I don't—"

"No thanks necessary. They'll be over in a little while to work off their debt." Ms. Myrna turned to go.

Mrs. Price tried again. "But I actually have plenty of help, Myrna."

"You can never have too much help!" she yelled, waddling down the sidewalk.

Nobody said a word as we watched the old woman shuffle across the street.

I pulled on Mrs. Price's sleeve. "Please tell me this means Ernie and Bernie will be taking our place tonight and we won't even be here."

Mrs. Price took a deep breath. "No, Bitsy, I'm afraid it means we all have to learn to work together. At least for one night."

I spoke for everyone. "Grief!"

Before we knew it, Garrett, Ellie, and I were in the kitchen, washing dishes. It was hopeless trying to work out a system with Ernie and Bernie. The original plan was that some of us would walk among the guests and gather dirty dishes while the others stayed in the kitchen, washing, drying, and putting the clean things back on the serving table.

But the plan wasn't working. The twins would go out to get dirty dishes and come back with only one or two plates, while their pockets and mouths were stuffed with cookies and brownies and cheesecake. I could tell they weren't concerned about eating healthy at all.

"Here's our peace offering."

We turned from the sink to see Ernie holding out two cups of punch for Garrett and me. Bernie handed a cup to Ellie. We hesitated.

"What's the matter?" Ernie asked. "Afraid we'll poison you or something?" He laughed and set the drinks on the kitchen table. "Suit yourself." He shoved me away from the sink. "Get out of the way. It's our turn to wash."

I watched him over my shoulder, took a few steps toward the hall, and crashed into two men coming in through the back door. "Excuse me," we all said together.

Screech! Mooshew flapped his wings and soared to the ceiling, finally landing on the curtain rod.

The men didn't say anything else, just headed down the hall to join the adults. We must have crashed harder than I thought, because one of the men was limping.

Garrett glared at Ernie. "See what you've done? Mooshew's not used to people pushing each other. We don't do that around here." Garrett stuck his nose in the air and started toward the hall. Ellie and I copied him.

"I guess you know your house is haunted," Ernie announced from his position at the sink.

We stopped, our backs to the twins.

"Ernie!" Bernie said.

"It is. Has been ever since those nuns took in all

those sick people. It was a dumb thing to do. Should've just let 'em all die."

In a flash, Garrett was at the sink, standing face-to-face with the bully. "It wasn't dumb, it was brave." The words tumbled out fast, like he was afraid to stop. "Of course, you'd never understand that, would you? All you think about is yourself and what you want and how you're going to get it. For your information, our house is not haunted because of those nuns, it's *protected* because of them." He poked his finger in Ernie's chest. "It's protected from the likes of you." With that, my friend headed to the living room. "Come on, girls, we've got work to do."

Ellie and I silently followed him out of the kitchen until we reached the crowded foyer. "Way to go, Garrett," I whispered, holding up my hand for a high five. But no high fives were coming. "What's wrong?"

"He really knows how to turn things around, doesn't he?" Garrett said. "I can't believe how he can take something as wonderful as the history of this house and turn it into a joke."

"So there really were some nuns?" I asked.

He shook his head. "Bitsy, I can't believe you've been here three days and haven't read the marker in front of our house. It tells the whole story."

I knew the sign was out there, but I hadn't taken the time to read it. "Uh, I was going to. Later. You want to just tell me the story and save me the time?"

Garrett rolled his eyes. "I guess I could give you the short version. Back in 1875, the Catholic Church bought this house to be a home and school for the Sisters of St. Joseph, a group of nuns. But in 1877 there was an outbreak of yellow fever on Amelia Island, and the nuns used their house—our house—as a hospital."

I surveyed the beautiful wallpaper and colorful paintings. "This house was a hospital?"

"Yep. Didn't matter what color or what religion the sick people were, the sisters took care of everybody, day and night, for three weeks. In the end, a bunch of people on the island died, including two of the nuns."

My eyes studied the foyer and tried to imagine the sights, sounds, and smells of the sick, piled on top of each other, calling for help and healing. I could see the nuns, tired from days without sleep, running from one patient to the next, offering water and prayer. "Wow, what a story. So that's why you have a picture of nuns at the top of your stairs."

"Yeah, we don't want to forget what this house—and those nuns—meant to a lot of people."

"But what's this about a ghost?"

"I don't know," Garrett said. "I've never heard anything about that. But whatever it is, I don't believe it. Come on, we'd better get to work."

We piled up the dirty dishes and made our way through the crowd. We walked into the kitchen, set the dishes on the green counter, and left without saying a word.

Once we were back in the foyer, Ellie said, "Can you believe how slow those two are at washing dishes?" She scanned the living room. "Looks like they won't have to wash very many, either. Most people are just standing around talking now. I knew we'd end up doing all of the work."

And that's when it hit me—the best idea I'd had in a long, long time! I pulled Garrett and Ellie over to the corner and whispered my plan. Their smiles told me they agreed.

Ellie headed to the living room and grabbed the few dirty dishes still sitting on the table, while Garrett and I ran to the dining room. We waited for a man and woman to fill their plates and leave, then we each picked up a clean plate and smeared it with ranch dressing, sprinkled it with crumbs, and tossed in a crinkled napkin. Then we did it again and again, piling the dishes in a stack. Ellie entered with her own collection, and we walked the few steps to the kitchen.

"What? More dishes?" Ernie said, wiping his face with his shirt sleeve. "I didn't agree to all this."

"I don't think you really had a choice, Ernie," I said. "Now, get back to work, or I'm calling Mrs. Price." Then I turned and walked out. My friends followed me.

Next, Ellie and I lined up punch cups, poured a little in each one, and slurped it down, while Garrett dipped clean forks in the dressing and licked it off. Pretty soon, we had another impressive collection.

"Let's go," I whispered.

We marched single file through the crowd and put the dishes on the kitchen counter.

"Hey, enough already," Bernie said.

"Sorry," Garrett answered. "Should've thought of that before you stole the box."

We walked straight to the dining room and prepared our next sabotage. Ellie poured the punch, Garrett licked the forks, and I crumbled the cookies on the plate. We'd begun packing up our next round of dishes when we heard a noise behind us.

"Having fun?"

We turned around to see Ernie leaning against the wall, slinging a wet towel in his pruney hand. I took off running first, Garrett and Ellie right behind me. We dashed out of the dining room and elbowed our way through the foyer. We tried to go upstairs, but the steps were too crowded, so we headed to the living room instead. There we found Mr. and Mrs. Price standing in front of the fireplace. We hid behind them.

"What are you doing?" Mrs. Price whispered. "Go away, you're being rude."

I led the way to the foyer and peeked around the corner in time to see the twins push their way up the stairs. I turned to Garrett and Ellie and said, "Follow me."

We politely stepped around the adults and headed to

the back of the house. "Here!" I led the way into their parents' bedroom across from the kitchen, threw open the closet doors, and squeezed my way between the clothes, my friends right behind me. I put my finger to my lips. "Shhh!"

Within seconds, we heard the door squeak open and shut. I hoped Ernie and Bernie couldn't hear my heart pounding. A second later, we heard another squeak.

"Whew!" I whispered. "They're gone." But before we could move, we heard voices.

"So, did you get it?" a deep voice said. It didn't sound like one of the twins.

"Um, no, sir. I looked over the fireplace, just like you said, but it weren't there." The voices seemed metallic, like something over a walkie-talkie.

"Well, did you try looking anywhere else?"

"Oh, yes, sir. I looked all over the house, but it weren't nowhere."

"Hmm," the first voice said. "It's got to be somewhere. Guess we'll have to leave it up to the ghost."

I grabbed my friends' arms and sucked in a big breath.

"S-sir?" the second voice said. "Did you say g-ghost?"

"Oh, never mind. Look, that's all I need. How much do I owe you?"

"But . . . but is that ghost going to hurt me?"

"No, no. Don't worry about it. Now, what do I owe you?" the man asked again.

"Oh, it weren't no trouble, sir. I . . . I just like to help people." I could hear the smile in his voice.

"Whatever," the deep voice said.

"Let me know if I can help you again," the nice man said. "I mean it. I like to help people."

"Sure. Don't mention it." The man paused. "Actually, don't mention it to anybody. Now, you stay here until I get out the door, then you can leave after I'm gone. Got it?"

"Y-yes, sir. Thank you, sir."

My friends and I listened as a door squeaked open and shut. A few seconds later, it did it again. We stepped all over each other trying to get out of the closet. I pushed through first and fell into the room, landing with a *plop,* right at Ernie's feet!

"What are—"

But before the rest of my words could come out, Ernie said, "Did you hear that?"

Bernie stood beside him, her face pale. Garrett and Ellie stumbled out of the closet and gasped.

I answered Ernie. "What do you mean, did I hear that? You were in here. Didn't you see them? Who was it?"

"It wasn't anybody," Ernie said. "It came from that." He pointed to a plastic box on the dresser.

"The boys' room!" Ellie yelled as she ran out the door. Ernie, Bernie, Garrett, and I followed her through the crowded foyer, up the packed staircase, and around the upstairs mass of people to the boys' bedroom. Ellie threw open the door. The room was empty.

I led the way into the room, closed the door behind us, and grabbed Ernie's arm. "Okay, somebody tell me what's going on."

"Don't look at me," he said. "I'm as confused as you are."

Then Garrett took over. "So you guys didn't see anybody come into my parents' room?"

"No," Ernie answered. "Bernie and I saw you go in, so we came in behind you and closed the door. That's when we heard the door close, you know, over the speaker-thing."

"It's a monitor," Ellie corrected. "See, you put one part in the room with the baby, and the other part goes in the parents' room. That way they can hear if the baby cries."

Bernie threw her hands in the air. "I don't care about how the thing works, just tell me what happened. Who was that? What were they talking about?"

"That's what I want to know," Garrett said.

"That's what we *all* want to know," Ernie added.

Garrett paused, raised his eyebrows, and looked around at each of us. "This is really weird."

"What's weird?" I said.

"Looks like we're all on the same team here."

"Uh, I guess it does," Ernie said. Then he smiled. "That's a switch, huh?"

I rubbed my hand across my damaged face and flinched from the pain. "Yeah, quite a switch."

"Well, if we really are on the same team," Garrett said, "we'd better start working together." He turned to Ernie. "Are you in? For real?"

"For real."

Garrett looked at Bernie.

"Me, too," she said.

"Count me in," Ellie said, moving to Bernie's side.

Within seconds, my scraped knees and elbows were screaming their disapproval. I forced my right eyelid open and looked at Ernie with both eyes. "Okay, but this better not be a trick."

CHAPTER · 10

THE FIVE OF US SAT AROUND THE KITCHEN TABLE AND planned our next move—to spread out among the visitors, listen to the voices, and see if we could figure out who we'd heard over the monitor. The girls headed to the living room, while the guys went back upstairs and mingled.

We strolled into the room like we were supposed to be there. I saw two men and two women standing by the coffee table. Ellie pointed to the younger man. "The mayor," she whispered.

I recognized the older man. He was the one I'd bumped into in the kitchen—the one with the limp.

The mayor spoke to the older man. "How do you like it here . . . uh . . . excuse me, what did you say your name was?"

"Norman. Norman Bridges. Oh, it's a lovely little town. I've always loved it."

"So, you're from Amelia?" the older woman asked.

"No, no, just here for the auction. I like to dabble in antiques, but I own a Circuit Shack in St. Augustine. My mother used to live here. I visited her once."

The lady stepped closer. "Oh, really? What was her name? Maybe I knew her."

I could tell we were getting nowhere with this conversation, so I motioned to Ellie and Bernie. We pretended to clear the dishes as we moved over to Mr. Ed, who was talking to a short man with a big belly.

Ellie leaned over and whispered, "That's Mr. Shorty, the man who owns the grocery store."

I nodded my understanding.

Mr. Shorty was talking. "It's all so unfair. I can't believe my own uncle won't let me have anything from the house. It's not like I'm asking for much. And I *am* the only living relative, you know."

"I can see why you'd be upset," Mr. Ed answered.

"Upset? I'm ready to choke somebody!"

"I bet you are." Mr. Ed ran his hand over his shaved head. "Hey, you never did answer my question. What do I owe you?"

Bernie, Ellie, and I stopped in our tracks.

"Nothing, Ed," Mr. Shorty said. "It was fun. I enjoyed it."

A plate slipped from Bernie's hand and shattered on the floor. Ellie and I rushed to her.

"Here, let me help," Mr. Ed said. He gathered the pieces and placed them in the trash.

"Th-thanks, Mr. Ed," I said.

"Don't mention it."

All three of us sucked in a big breath and ran out of the room. The guys were coming down the stairs, so I pointed them to the kitchen.

We all tried to talk at once. I put my hands up to get control of the situation. "Go ahead, Ellie."

"It was Mr. Shorty we heard on the monitor. He said himself he was ready to choke someone."

"No, it's not," Bernie chimed in. "It's Mr. Ed. Didn't you hear what he said?"

I shook my head. "I heard him. But he's our friend. He'd never sic a ghost on us."

Garrett reported next. "Well, we saw Mr. Robison from the jewelry store and Mr. Brown, the man who works at the library. Neither one of their voices sounded like what we heard over the speaker, but it's hard to tell. Oh, and we also saw Ricky, and Daddy's friend Mr. Johnny, but we're sure they wouldn't be the ones. We didn't know the rest of the people."

"We don't even know if the bad guys are still here," Ernie said. "They could be long gone by now."

My voice dropped to a bare whisper. "You're probably right."

Mrs. Price stuck her head in the kitchen. "Hey, what's the holdup in here?"

"Uh, sorry, Mom," Garrett said. "We'll be done in a few minutes."

His mom returned to her guests.

"Let's figure it out while we work," I said, reaching for one of the punch cups the twins had brought in earlier. "Guess I'll help by getting rid of this." I tipped the drink to my mouth.

"Wait!" Ernie yelled, grabbing my arm.

"What?"

"You . . . uh . . . you might not want to drink that."

I went to the sink, poured the punch down the drain, and examined the cup. There, in the bottom, was a glob of ranch dressing. I squinted at the twins. "I knew you couldn't be trusted."

Ernie joined me at the sink. "Bitsy, that was before our truce, remember?"

"Sorry," Bernie said, putting her arm around my shoulders. "Friends?"

As far as it depends on me. . . . I smiled, remembering the Bible verse, but my heart didn't feel it. "Friends," I muttered.

We discussed our problem while we finished the kitchen. By the time the last fork was dried, we knew we couldn't share our story with anyone. Not yet.

Mr. Price came in and sat at the table. "Well, what's your secret?"

"S-sir?" Ellie and Bernie said together.

"What do you mean?" I asked, trying to sound innocent. "We don't have a secret."

Mr. Price laughed. "Don't be so suspicious. It's a

compliment. I just want to know your secret for working so well together."

We all faked a laugh, and I said, "Oh, I . . . I guess we just had to get to know each other better."

The gang agreed.

"I think you're right, Bitsy. The whole world could probably get along if we got to know each other better." He stood. "Oh, Garrett, I almost forgot. Ed wanted me to tell you he likes the new paint job in your bedroom."

None of us moved a muscle as we watched Mr. Price leave the room.

Mooshew flapped his wings and squawked.

CHAPTER · 11

I KNEW BEFORE MY HEAD HIT THE PILLOW THAT I would have trouble falling asleep that night. There were too many questions. Then I remembered reading that making a list of your concerns helps clear your mind. I decided it was definitely worth a try.

Ellie snorted as I lifted the cover and slid out of bed. I tiptoed to the desk, turned on the light, grabbed a purple marker and a sheet of notebook paper, and started my list:

1. Who did we hear on the monitor? Mr. Ed? Mr. Shorty? Mr. Robison?

2. What would a ghost have to do with this house? With the nuns?

3. Who would send the ghost? Answer: the man on the monitor.

Trooper barked outside.

4. How am I going to get well in time for the talent show?

Mooshew squawked downstairs. I stopped writing and looked up. Trooper barked another warning.

"Ellie, get up," I whispered, running to the bed. "Something's wrong outside!"

She sat up and rubbed her eyes. "What—?"

"Listen!"

Trooper and Mooshew were getting louder with every passing moment.

"Come on, let's get Garrett!" I said, pulling my friend out of bed.

We grabbed our robes and ran across the hall. I stopped at the door and put my finger over my lips and then pointed to the baby monitor. Ellie got the message.

I reached Garrett's bed first and tapped his arm. "Wh—" he started, but I covered his mouth before he could say a word. Ellie pointed at the monitor and then motioned for him to follow us out the door. I removed my hand only after he nodded his understanding.

We tiptoed out of the bedroom, down the stairs, and past their parents' closed door. Trooper barked and Mooshew squawked as Garrett undid the lock. We slipped out the back door.

"Oo-oo-oo."

We grabbed each other on the dark porch.

"What was that?" Ellie asked.

Mooshew squawked again.

"OO-OO-OO." Louder this time!

"Could that be the . . . the ghost?" I asked.

"Bitsy, get real," Garrett said, looking over my head at the creepy house next door.

"I'm trying. But this all seems pretty real to me."

"Me, too," Ellie said.

Garrett stretched his neck. "What's that?"

"What?" I asked, looking up at him.

He pointed across the yard to Mr. Hawkins's house and said, "That."

I couldn't believe my eyes, but there it was—a real, live ghost—shining through the window of the creepy house.

Garrett, Ellie, and I screamed at the top of our lungs and grabbed for each other in the darkness. Within seconds, the porch light was on, and Ellie's mom and dad were with us, holding us as we cried.

"It was a ghost!" Ellie shouted.

"A real one," I added. "We heard it. We saw it!"

Garrett just stood there, wiping his eyes.

"Now, now," Mrs. Price said, stroking my hair and Ellie's.

Mr. Price held Garrett close.

"What's going on?" a voice called from the yard.

Ellie and I held tighter to her mom.

Mr. Ed reached the porch, the light revealing his face. Trooper was beside him, bouncing like he was on a trampoline.

Ellie's dad turned to Mr. Ed and said, "The kids say

they heard a noise and saw something in the window next door."

It was good to have a daddy around.

"Hmm." Mr. Ed scratched his head. "I figured something was up, because Trooper was having a fit. Then I heard the screams."

At that moment, Ernie and Bernie ran to the porch. I pulled away from Mrs. Price and quickly wiped my eyes.

"Did y'all hear that?" Ernie asked. "Did you see it?"

"Yeah," Garrett and Ellie said.

"Wasn't it cool?" I added.

Garrett and his family looked at me. Ellie rolled her eyes.

"You could hear something all the way over at your house?" Mrs. Price asked.

"Well," Bernie said, "we were out on the porch, waiting for Aunt Myrna. She's working second shift tonight."

"You were there by yourselves?" Mrs. Price reached over and put her hand on Bernie's shoulder. "You poor things."

Bernie shrugged. "It's okay. We do it all the time."

"Well, I don't think it's a good idea," Ellie's mom said. "You know you're always welcome to stay with us."

"Or at least let me know you're alone," Mr. Ed added, "so I can check on you." Then he turned to Mrs. Price. "Isn't the power still off over there?"

She nodded.

"What about the key?" he asked.

"I let Marsha take it so she could work over there tomorrow," she answered.

"Okay, wait here," he said, taking off for the creepy house.

"See, I was right," Bernie said. "It's him."

"It is not!" I shouted.

"Whoa, wait a minute," Mrs. Price said. "Who's what?"

Garrett cut his eyes at me and then at Ellie. "I'll tell you, Mom, but you're not going to like it."

"Try me," she said.

We told her about the monitor, the voices, and the conversation about the ghost. Bernie even shared her suspicions about Mr. Ed.

Mrs. Price tucked a yellow curl behind her ear. "So you think Mr. Ed wants to steal something from our house, and he's sending a ghost because he can't find it?"

"Well, not really," Bernie said. "We aren't sure who's doing it yet."

Mr. Ed walked up. "Who's doing what?"

We plopped down on the porch steps and told everything again, which, when you hear yourself tell it, doesn't sound like very much.

"And you think it's me?" Mr. Ed shook his head and rubbed the back of his neck. "I thought you knew me better than that."

I stood and hugged the retired policeman. "We do, Mr. Ed. We're sorry."

Garrett, Ellie, and the twins joined me at his side.

"Apology accepted, even though it still hurts"—he pointed at his chest—"right here." He stood. "But there is a problem over there. A window's busted out."

Ernie looked at his sister. "Um, that one's our fault. We did that yesterday . . . before—"

"Before we were friends," Garrett interrupted.

Bernie said, "We really are sorry, Mr. Ed."

He smiled. "Okay. But, about this ghost thing, I didn't see or hear anything. Trooper woke me up barking, and then I heard the screams and saw the lights come on. So I can't really say what happened. Do you want me to call the chief?"

"Yes!" we all answered together.

"I don't know, Ed," Mr. Price said. "We don't really have much to tell him."

"We do, too!" I yelled.

"What are you going to say?" Mr. Price asked. "That you saw a ghost?"

"We *did* see a ghost!" Ellie said.

"No, you saw a light and you heard a noise. That's a long way from seeing and hearing a ghost." He faced the policeman. "Ed, why don't you and I take another look when it's daylight? I'd hate to start a bunch of ghost rumors. You know how people are."

"Sounds like a good idea." Mr. Ed turned to us.

"Look, I understand your concern, but whatever you do, don't mention the ghost to anyone else."

We agreed.

Mr. Ed started back across the street, Trooper running in circles around him.

Ernie and Bernie got ready to leave, but Mrs. Price motioned toward the steps. "Could you wait a minute?"

The twins sat down, and we sat beside them.

Mrs. Price leaned over on her elbows and addressed each of us. "There's something I'm concerned about. You know, in the Bible we're told that there really are spirits of good and evil. The problem is, sometimes it's hard to tell which is which." A chill ran down my back. "Something that may seem like only a game to us could potentially be very wicked. That's why we're warned to avoid anything that could have an evil influence. We could be dealing with much more than we realize."

Garrett glanced around at the rest of us and then asked, "You mean . . . this talk about a ghost?"

"That's exactly what I mean. I think it's best if you stay away from all this ghost stuff."

We all eyed each other and nodded our heads.

Ernie and Bernie got up again, but this time Bernie stepped over to Mrs. Price, hugged her, and said, "Thank you." Then she jumped off the porch and walked with her brother into the dark night.

CHAPTER · 12

NEEDLESS TO SAY, WE DIDN'T GET MUCH SLEEP THAT night, so we were groggy the next morning. I surveyed my injuries while Ellie brushed her teeth.

"My face certainly looks better," I said. "At least I can open my eye all the way."

"Yeah, you can open it to see the black circle around it."

I looked in the mirror at my friend. "Thanks for the encouragement. But for your information, that's not a black circle. I have deep-set eyes, and that's good."

"Um-hum."

I could tell she didn't believe me. "It's true. People pay good money to have eyes like mine."

"Sure, Bitsy. If you say so."

"Well, I am walking better, don't you think? And the scabs on my knees and elbows aren't draining anymore."

"Bit-sy!" Ellie singsonged. "Will you stop it? You're going to make me throw up!"

"See, I knew blondes were girly-girls," I shot back.

"What about Garrett? Do you think he's a sissy?"

"Of course not. It doesn't work with boys." I studied my reflection in the mirror. "Oh, I hope my hair's blonde by Saturday." I brushed out my brown curls under the bathroom light. "Can you tell a difference yet?"

Ellie leaned over and studied my hair. "Nope, don't think so."

I grabbed the bottle of Sun-Glow. "Well, this'll help it along."

"Hey, you're only supposed to use it when you're going to be out in the sun. You're just wasting money."

"No, I'm not. I'm going to be in the sun, as soon as breakfast is over."

"You are?"

"Didn't you say you have to take refreshments for your youth group tonight?"

"Yeah. . . ."

"Well, we'll get the twins and walk to the store for refreshments while we work on our mystery at the same time. We'll kill two birds with one stone. No, three—I forgot the Sun-Glow in my hair."

Ellie scrunched her eyes. "Who said anything about killing birds?"

"Never mind. Come on, let's eat."

We ran down the stairs and into the kitchen. Ellie scarfed down a Pop-Tart, while I chewed my vitamin and ate raisin bran and milk. Had it been only twenty-four hours since I started this health routine? Well, at least I could tell it was working. Things were going to be great by the time the talent show rolled around on Saturday.

Garrett stumbled in, rubbing his eyes. "What are y'all doing up so early?"

Before we could answer, Mrs. Price came in the back door, carrying Nicolas. "Your dad and Mr. Ed didn't find anything except the broken window, so I guess there's no need to file a report." She put the baby down.

"Are you sure?" I asked.

"Yes, we'll keep an eye out for anything else unusual." She poured juice into a sippy cup, grabbed Nicolas, and headed toward the door.

"Wait, Mom," Ellie said. "Is it okay if we walk to Shorty's and get the snacks for youth group tonight?"

Garrett was suddenly awake. "Walk?"

"You want to walk?" their mother asked.

"Yes, ma'am," Ellie answered. "And we want to take Ernie and Bernie with us. Maybe they could go to youth group with us, too."

"Are you serious? How nice," Mrs. Price replied. "Sure, go ahead. Just be careful—"

"We know," Garrett said. "We'll be careful crossing the street. Mom, we're not babies, you know."

"Well, being careful crossing the street is important,

but I was going to say be careful not to mention the ghost to anyone. Remember what Mr. Ed said about starting rumors."

"Oh," Garrett said. "Don't worry. We're trying to forget all about ghosts."

The sun was shining bright when we hit the sidewalk and headed toward the grocery store. I was glad I'd added that extra dose of Sun-Glow. *My hair should be getting lighter anytime now,* I thought.

I looked over at my new friend and checked out his wounded face. "You know, Ernie, your injuries would get well faster if you ate healthy food, took some vitamins, and eliminated all the fat and sugar from your diet. That's what I'm doing."

He stopped walking and gave my face a once-over. "Is that so?" Then he ran ahead to walk beside Garrett, who changed the subject.

"I'm getting concerned about Mooshew," Garrett said. "He's been acting weird lately."

"What's he doing?" Ernie asked.

"I don't know, kind of moping around. Like something's bothering him."

Ernie whispered. "Could it be . . . the ghost?" He laughed and took off running.

We all ran the rest of the way to the grocery store, where Garrett held the door for all us girls. I was impressed, even though I wasn't sure if that meant he thought I was a girly-girl or something. Once we got inside, we grabbed a cart and started down the snack aisle.

"Hey, isn't this where you said that guy Ricky works?" I asked.

"Yeah," Garrett answered. "Maybe you could meet him, then you'd see why we're so excited about the resource center."

We headed straight for the chips and were studying the selection when we heard a man in the next aisle. "Someone at the post office told me that it was a woman ghost and she had a knife in her hand."

Ellie started to speak, but I put my finger to my lips and did the "quiet" sign.

"A woman?" a lady said. "Could it be that nun? But why would a nun have a knife in her hand? And why would she be at Hawkins's house? That doesn't make sense."

Then the man spoke again. "Sounds like that house is haunted, if you ask me. You'd never catch me inside it, that's for sure. Probably won't have any clients show up for the resource center, either. Or worse, what if people do go and something happens to somebody? They'd sue the city for everything it owns! I'm telling you, the resource center isn't a good idea. Amelia Island had better reconsider this offer."

We stood still as the voices got farther and farther away.

Garrett spoke up first. "Okay, Ernie . . . Bernie, which one of you did it? Which one of you told about the ghost?"

Bernie shoved away from the grocery cart. "How dare you? How dare you accuse us? Come on, Ernie. We don't need friends like this."

Ernie grabbed his sister's arm. "Hold up a minute, Bernie." Then he faced us. "Look, if you don't believe you can trust us, then we just need to go home. Bernie's right. We don't need friends this bad."

I knew I had to take control of the situation before it totally fell apart. "Look, guys, Garrett's sorry, aren't you, Garrett?" He didn't answer, so I continued. "We're all sorry. We really are. But you have to remember, this friendship thing is new to us, too. We hardly know you."

Bernie rolled her eyes.

I tried again. "I promise, from this moment on, we're going to treat you like friends."

The twins looked at each other and then back at us. Ernie spoke for both of them. "Are you sure y'all want to be friends? Real friends?"

Garrett and Ellie nodded their heads.

"I do," I said. And this time I meant it.

A few minutes later, with enough chips, dip, salsa, and nuts to feed a church full of hungry kids, we headed to the checkout line. Mr. Shorty and another man had their backs to us, but their voices were pretty loud.

There was no doubt about Mr. Shorty's feelings. "Like I told Ed last night, this whole thing just gets me. Here I am, Hawkins's only living relative, and I can't even bid on one single thing out of that house. Can you believe it?"

"That is a shame," the man said.

Was that the same voice we had heard in the aisle? I wasn't sure.

Mr. Shorty continued. "I don't want much, just the family portrait that used to hang over the fireplace."

We all took in a big breath.

The fireplace? That's what we heard the men talking about on the monitor!

When I saw my friends' eyes pop open, I knew they were thinking the same thing. I pushed the cart a little closer.

Mr. Shorty was still talking. "Aw, I guess it doesn't really matter anyway. The picture's gone, from what I hear. But tell me this—why would Hawkins give a family portrait to somebody who's not even in the family?" The man clasped his hands around his big belly. "Sure would like to have that picture with my mama in it . . . God rest her soul."

Garrett started to say something, but the stranger spoke up. "Well, I think you deserve it more than anybody. And for that reason, I'll tell you what I'm going to do. If that picture shows up, I'll bid on it for you. All you have to do is give me the money. I'll place the bid, and nobody'll know the difference. That way you won't have to worry about someone else getting it."

Mr. Shorty turned toward the man, and we could see his face light up. "Really? You'd do that for me?"

"It's only fair. That picture rightly belongs to you. It's part of your heritage. It'd be a shame to see it go to anybody else."

"Thanks, Norman. How could I ever repay you?" Mr. Shorty grabbed the man's hand and pumped it up and down.

Norman? Where've I heard that name before? I thought. *And that's the third time somebody's talked about paying somebody.*

"There's no need to repay me. All you have to do is find that picture."

Mr. Shorty turned and jumped when he saw us. We jumped, too.

"Oh, sorry," he said. "I didn't know I had any customers in the store."

The stranger limped out the door.

It took a second for me to realize I was going to have to speak for the group. "Oh, that's okay. We haven't been here long." I aimed the cart into the checkout line. *What else can I talk about?* "Uh, is Ricky working today? We didn't see him while we were shopping."

"No," Mr. Shorty answered as he rang up our groceries. "His mama had to take him to a doctor's appointment today. Don't expect he'll be in at all."

Then he stopped checking the groceries and studied me over his glasses. "I don't believe I know you. What's your name?"

"Bitsy."

"Well, Bitsy, since he's not here, is there something I could do for you?"

"Oh, no, sir. I just wanted to tell Ricky hello."

We paid, grabbed the groceries, and rushed out the door.

"What was that all about?" Ellie asked. "Was Mr. Shorty the one we heard on the monitor? He must have been looking for that picture over the fireplace!"

Ernie cleared his throat and shuffled his feet. "Uh . . . Bernie and I might know something about that picture."

"What?" we asked together.

"Well," he said, "there was some sort of picture in that box we took from Mr. Hawkins's house. It had a family on it."

"What?" I said again.

"We just grabbed the closest box. We didn't care what was in it."

"Why haven't you told us this before?" I asked. "Friends don't keep secrets, remember?"

Bernie stepped up to me, but her face was kind. "We weren't keeping secrets, Bitsy, it just never came up. To be honest, I'd forgotten about the box. Aunt Myrna said she was going to return it."

"Nobody's said anything about a picture until now," Ernie said. "How could we have known what they were talking about?"

"They're right, Bitsy," Garrett said. "The question is, what are we going to do about it now that we do know?"

"First, we'll check at our house and see if we can find it," Ernie said. "Aunt Myrna's been working so much, she probably just forgot about it."

I agreed. We walked in silence, but my mind never slowed down. After a few minutes, I said, "But that still doesn't explain the part about the ghost. Why would Mr. Shorty send a ghost?"

"I know," Bernie said. "What if he was trying to scare the person who had the picture? Maybe he was trying to scare them into bringing it back."

Ernie ran his hand through his spiked hair. "Maybe so."

"But that's not all," I said. "The ghost must have been meant for the five of us. We're the only ones who live close enough to see it." I turned to Ernie. "Could Mr. Shorty have known you had it?"

Ernie's eyes got as big as saucers. "I bet you're right. He knows."

"Of course I'm right." I smiled and held my arms out like a queen to her servants. "I'm always right."

"Don't be so humble, Bitsy," Garrett said, jabbing my arm. "It's not like you."

We all laughed and continued down the sidewalk. The sun felt good against the sore muscles in my back. And I knew the warm sun was good for my hair, too. Only three more days and I'd be a blonde. Then I'd know if blondes really do have more fun.

CHAPTER · 13

WE WERE ALMOST TO THE PRICES' YELLOW HOUSE WHEN Trooper saw us. Before we knew it, he was jumping and licking, circling our feet, and announcing our arrival.

I put the groceries on the sidewalk, knelt down, and rubbed his ears. "Why don't you solve this mystery for us, Trooper? That's what police dogs are for."

"He's retired," Ellie said.

"So? He still has what it takes. It's in his blood."

"Hi, guys," Mr. Ed said, putting on his green ball cap as he came out the front door of Ellie's house. "I'm glad you made it back before I left. Just wanted to tell you how much I appreciated all your help with the open house last night."

"You're welcome," Garrett said.

"How much do I owe you?"

I tried to swallow the lump in my throat. "S-sir?"

"You all did a great job, and I'd like to reward you for it. How much do I owe you?"

"Oh, it was nothing," Ernie said. "We like helping people."

We all jerked our heads to look at Ernie. *Did he just say what I think he said?*

"Well, I tell you what," the retired policeman said. "I'll be filling in for Ronnie at the ice cream parlor Thursday night. Come by then, and I'll treat you to the flavor of your choice."

Ernie's face lit up like a Christmas tree. "Really?"

"Thanks, Mr. Ed," Garrett said. "Maybe my dad can bring us by when he goes to the Pogy Plant."

"Sounds like a plan. See you Thursday night." Mr. Ed turned to his Belgian shepherd and whistled. Trooper raced ahead, grabbed a tennis ball from his front yard, and circled back. The man took the ball, stopped, and turned to us. "Oh, I almost forgot, I have one more question. You kids didn't tell anybody about the ghost, did you?"

"No, sir," we answered together.

"Good." He threw the ball and followed Trooper across the street.

"What's the po . . . po—" I started.

"The Pogy Plant," Garrett said. "It's an industrial park over by the Amelia River. Mr. Johnny's business is there."

Ernie's voice was soft. "Your dad goes there at night?"

"Sure. He meets with Mr. Johnny and another friend, Mr. Bill, every Thursday night to pray. Why?"

"Has he ever seen . . . the witch?"

"The what?" I asked.

"The witch," Ernie said. "The Pogy Witch Woman."

I threw my hands in the air. "Here we go again."

"No, it's true," Ernie said. "I've seen it. There's this witch that lives in the woods at the Pogy Plant. If you see a light come on in the woods, it's her. She's lighting her lantern. That means she's coming to get you."

I wasn't buying that story. "That's ridiculous. Besides, this is exactly what Mrs. Price was talking about yesterday."

"No," Ernie said, "she was talking about ghosts. This is a witch."

"Ghosts. Witches. It's all the same thing," Garrett said. "Mom says we need to stay away from it."

"And that's exactly what I'm doing," Ernie said. "You won't catch me over there Thursday night—or any other night."

Garrett stepped up to the porch. "Fine. That means more ice cream for me!"

CHAPTER · 14

WE WERE GETTING READY FOR YOUTH GROUP WHEN I grabbed Ellie's arm and pulled her to the mirror. "Look at my hair. I think it looks a little lighter."

She rotated my head back and forth under the bathroom lights. Then she brushed her fingers through my curls. "I'm not sure. What do you think, Bernie?"

Bernie repeated Ellie's motions. "I don't know. It looks different, but I'm not sure it looks lighter."

I pulled away from my friends and headed back to the bedroom. "I can't believe you don't see it. It's definitely blonder." Grabbing my business shoebox from the closet, I plopped on the bed, removed the box lid, and straightened the necklaces.

"Wow!" Bernie said. "Where'd you get those?"

I pointed to the gold "B" hanging from my neck.

"How beautiful," she said.

"Thanks." I picked up the box. "This is my stock. I have my own business. It's called Bitsy's Bangles."

"Your own business? How cool!"

"It is pretty cool, isn't it? My dad helped me get started, but now it's all mine."

She bent over for a closer look at my initial. "Hey, that could stand for Bernie," she said.

"I guess it could, but mine stands for Bitsy. You could buy one if you want. They're only five dollars."

She sat up straight and didn't say anything.

"That reminds me, Bernie," I said. "We know Ernie's real name is Ernest, what's yours—Bernest?" I laughed, but Ellie clenched her jaws and gave me a stern look.

Bernie lowered her head. "No, it's . . . it's Bernadette . . . after my mom."

My stomach did a flip-flop. I put my hand on Bernie's arm. "I'm sorry. I didn't mean to make fun of your name, or your mom's."

"That's okay. I just haven't thought about her in a few days, especially since we became friends. I think of her a lot when I'm lonely."

"What happened to your parents?" I asked.

Ellie gave me another dirty look. "Bitsy!"

"No, it's okay, Ellie. They died in a car accident. That's when we came to live with Aunt Myrna."

I wiped a tear from Bernie's cheek, then one from my own.

"Aunt Myrna's not mean or anything. She just doesn't have much time for us. All she does is work."

"I'm sorry, Bernie," I said, taking her into my arms.

She sniffled another second or two, then she sat up and wiped her eyes. "I'd better wash my face. I sure don't want to look bad the first time I go to church."

"Don't worry," Ellie said. "You'll look fine."

"But what if your friends don't like me?"

"What's not to like?" Ellie said. "Come on, I'll help you with your hair." They headed to the bathroom.

I picked up my shoe box and tried to imagine how many necklaces I would sell at church that night. *What will I do if I run out?* I wondered. *Will Daddy be able to send me some more?*

I got up from the bed and joined the girls in the bathroom. Ellie gathered the top of Bernie's hair and wrapped a clasp around it. "Perfect!" Ellie said.

"I agree!" I said. "Perfect!" Then I started to go.

"Oh, Bitsy, wait," Ellie said. "You need to wash your neck. You've got a little dirt"—she touched the side of my neck—"right there."

I reached in the cabinet for a clean washcloth, lathered it up, scrubbed, and rinsed. "Okay," I said, "let's go."

The youth group was pretty surprised to see us walk in with Ernie and Bernie, but Mr. and Mrs. Lyles welcomed them like old friends. Everyone else just stood back and watched. I think the group wanted to be sure the twins weren't going to sock someone in the nose or throw a snake in someone's face. But after a while, everybody realized the twins were okay, and before we knew it, Ernie and Bernie were part of the gang.

The band played and we all sang. I elbowed Garrett and said, "Hey, we've been singing for ten minutes, and the twins haven't banged our heads in beat to the music yet!"

He laughed.

Break time came, and all the girls clamored around me again as I headed to my bathroom office. Bernie just watched while Ellie tried to keep control.

"Okay, okay," Ellie said. "Everybody has to wait their turn. There's enough necklaces for everyone."

"And don't forget, I have matching earrings, too," I added. That's the difference between Ellie and me. She never considered that I had earrings to offer. *Daddy will be so proud of me and my business,* I thought. *Like father, like daughter.*

I had already sold three necklaces and a pair of earrings and was showing Camden a "C" when Ellie announced, "Attention everyone! I want you all to know that my friend Bitsy not only has her own jewelry business, but she's a television star, too!"

The girls stared at me. I could see the adoration in their eyes. "Well," I said, "I don't know if *star* is the right word."

But Ellie faced her friends and continued. "Okay, you tell me—how many of you have gotten a letter from a TV station, asking you to come in for an interview?"

She did have a point there. I didn't know anyone else but me who could say that.

"And you'll be able to see her perform live onstage at the July Fourth Talent Show this Saturday."

"Ellie!" I yelled. I didn't want anybody to see me in that ridiculous outfit, singing "I Enjoy Being a Girl."

The girls went crazy with questions.

"Quiet!" Ellie said. "We'll take one person at a time."

Several girls raised their hands.

"Yes?" Ellie pointed to a tall girl who had bought two necklaces.

"What's the name of your television show?"

I cleared my throat. "Actually, I don't have a show yet—"

"Are you in *People* magazine?" someone asked from the back of the line.

"Not yet."

Ellie put up her hands to silence the group. "Girls, girls, one at a time, please." Hands went up, and she pointed to a black-haired girl at the front of the line. "You may speak."

"Why's your neck dirty?"

I dropped the jewelry and covered my neck with my sweaty hand. "It's not dirt. My . . . my skin's just dark—I'm part Cherokee."

"I'm part Cherokee, too," the girl said. "But I don't look like I'm dirty."

Before I could think of an answer, Mrs. Lyles opened

the bathroom door. "Come on, girls. Break's over. Time to get started again." Her eyes followed the line of girls leading to my office on the sofa. "What are y'all doing in here, anyway?"

Ellie jumped to my defense. "Bitsy is selling some of her jewelry. Would you like to see it? She has an 'L.'"

"Uh, no, thank you. Girls, why don't you head on back to the group?"

Ellie, Bernie, and I gathered my things while Mrs. Lyles held the door for the girls. I put the lid on the shoe box, and we stood to go.

The teacher let the door close. "Could we talk a minute?"

"Yes, ma'am," Ellie and I said, keeping our eyes on our feet.

Bernie looked at us.

"You don't have to stay, Bernie," Mrs. Lyles said. She held the door for Bernie, then walked to the couch and patted its plaid surface. "Here, have a seat."

We did, and I decided this was a good timc to study my fingernails.

Mrs. Lyles crossed her hands in her lap and looked from Ellie's face to mine. "Do you think this is a good idea? Selling things at church?"

Ellic didn't say anything.

"I guess I never really thought about it," I said.

"Somehow, it just doesn't seem right for us to come to church to make money. What do you think?"

"I never really thought about it," I repeated, still studying my nails.

"Well, think about it this way. Some girls aren't going to have any money for jewelry. Couldn't that make them feel left out?"

We didn't answer.

"Plus, the saddest part is, it takes our minds off God and makes us think about money and things. Is that what you want?"

"Oh, no, ma'am!" I said. "That's not what I want at all!"

She smiled. "I didn't think so."

"I'm sorry. Really," I said.

"So, no more selling jewelry at church?"

"No, ma'am. I promise."

She patted my arm. "Thanks. I knew you'd understand." Then she stood. "Ready to get back to the group?"

"Yes, ma'am," Ellie and I said together.

Mrs. Lyles took a step as Ellie stood, but I just sat there. "Uh . . . we don't have to tell anybody about this, do we?" I asked.

The teacher took my hand. "Nope, sure don't. It's just between the three of us."

"Good," I said.

CHAPTER · 15

WE HAD A GREAT NIGHT. MR. LYLES TALKED ABOUT friendship and how real friends wouldn't talk us into doing bad things. We ended by praying for the strength to say no, and for the wisdom to choose good friends.

It seemed like only minutes had passed, but soon it was time to go. Ernie carried the bag of leftover snacks, and I had my shoe box of jewelry, as we headed down the sidewalk toward home. The girls walked on one side of me.

Garrett joined me on the other side and asked, "How'd your sales go?"

"Don't ask."

"Didn't sell much?"

"I did okay."

"Then what's the problem?"

"I don't want to talk about it."

He snorted. "Since when do you not want to talk about making money?"

I stomped my foot. "Since now!"

Garrett put up his hands like I was a bank robber or something. "Okay, okay," he said. "Forget that I said anything."

I held my head high and started back down the sidewalk.

We walked in silence for a few minutes, then Garrett said, "Ernie, I've been thinking about what you said. You know, about the ghost—the one at our house."

"Garrett!" Ellie said.

Ernie shook his head. "Forget it. It's nothing."

"It's not nothing to me," Garrett said. "It's my house. And it seems more real after what happened at Mr. Hawkins's house, and what those people said at the grocery store."

Ellie grabbed her brother's arm. "Garrett, remember what Mom said? Just forget it."

"I can't." He brushed off Ellie's hand and turned to Ernie. "So, what's the deal?"

"Well, I don't really know the whole story, but I do know that after the nuns died, they were buried on the property."

The three of us stopped and faced the twins. "You mean we have nuns buried in our yard?" Ellie asked.

"Oh, man," I said. "That's scary."

"No, wait a minute," Ernie said. "They aren't there anymore. Somebody moved 'em to the Bosque Bello Cemetery."

Ellie covered her mouth. "They dug up the bodies? Ewww!"

"Well, what does that have to do with a ghost?" Garrett asked Ernie. "You can't have a ghost without a dead body, can you?"

"I'm not sure about all the ghost rules," he said. "All I heard was that a nun rises up and walks into the church."

Ellie grabbed his arm. "Our church? The ghost walks into the First Baptist Church?"

"No, not your church. The nuns' church—St. Michael's."

"St. Michael's?" I asked.

"Yeah," Ernie said. "That's where you and I . . . uh, met the other day."

"Oh, yeah," I said, touching my damaged cheek.

"Anyway," Ernie continued, "all I know is, she rises up out of the cemetery and walks into the church."

"What cemetery? The one by St. Michael's?" I asked.

"Yeah, I guess," Ernie said. He moved the sack of groceries to his other arm. "Look, it's probably not even true. I wish I'd never said anything about it."

We took a few steps in silence, and then I stopped. "Let's check it out."

"What?" Ernie asked.

"Let's go to the cemetery and check it out," I suggested. "Find out firsthand."

"You're crazy!" Ellie said. "What would Mom say?"

"She won't know unless you tell her." My eyes burrowed into hers. "What's the matter? You chicken?"

Ellie watched her feet do nothing. "No."

"Come on, Ellie," Garrett said. "It won't take but a minute, and then we'll be done. Nobody'll ever know."

"Well—"

"Bernie, you in?" Ernie asked.

"I guess," she said, "but I don't like it either."

Girly-girls, I thought.

Ernie ignored his sister. "Everybody ready?"

We nodded in agreement and headed down the sidewalk. Pausing at the historical marker in front of the yellow house, we read the story of the nuns and their sacrifice, then walked another block to St. Michael's. Hiding behind a huge bush, we peered around the corner of the stucco building. In the middle of the churchyard was a tiny cemetery.

"That's it?" I asked. "That's all there is?"

"Yeah," Ernie said.

"Doesn't look like much of a cemetery to me."

"Well, maybe the people at this church don't die."

"Funny," I said, turning back toward the cemetery.

We waited and watched but didn't see a nun or any other kind of ghost rising from anywhere. We pulled back from the corner and squatted down on our heels.

"Guess we're not going to see anything tonight," Garrett said.

My ears tingled. "Shhh! What was that?"

"What?" they all asked.

"Quiet," I whispered. "Listen."

Scritch-scritch-scritch. Scritch-scritch-scritch.

The fear in my friends' eyes told me they'd heard it, too.

Ernie and I bounced back up and leaned around the corner. Garrett, Ellie, and Bernie shoved between us.

Then we saw it. A white body floated up from behind a grave marker, its white face waving with the breeze, a spear in its hand.

"The ghost!" I whispered loudly.

Ellie and Bernie screamed a duet as they fell on top of each other. Ernie threw down the grocery bag and fell over Garrett, who was scratching at the church wall, trying to get up. We all scrambled and fought to our feet, tripping and falling and rising again.

I was the last one up but the first one to reach the yellow house. I bounded up the steps two at a time, pushed through the door, and landed at Mrs. Price's feet, my shoe box still safe under my arm. Thc others fell in behind me. Ellie and Bernie cried, but the guys and I tried to explain what we saw.

"A ghost?" Mrs. Price asked.

"It was, Mommy, it was," Ellie cried.

Ellie's dad rushed down the stairs. "What in the world's going on?"

Mrs. Price held her daughter. "That's what I'm trying to find out. All right, somebody start at the beginning."

My eyes made a silent plea to Garrett. After all, it was *his* mom.

"Don't look at me," he said. "It was your idea."

It looked like it was up to me. Again. "Well, we wanted to see if there was a ghost—"

"Not we—you," Bernie interrupted. "*You* wanted to see if there was a ghost."

"But we all agreed—"

"We didn't agree—you made us," Bernie said, her arms folded across her chest.

"Made you? How could I—"

"Okay, that's enough," Mr. Price said. "Bitsy, just tell us what happened."

So I told them the story. I told them everything. About the nuns and the ghost story and the ghost we just saw and the people talking about ghosts at Shorty's. I even told them about Mr. Shorty wanting that picture, and that maybe he was the one we heard over the baby monitor.

"First of all," Mrs. Price said, "I don't think you have to worry about Shorty. And secondly, those ghost tales are just that—tales."

"But the man at Shorty's said there was a knife in the ghost's hand," I said. "Maybe it wasn't a knife after all. Maybe it was a spear. That's what it looked like to me."

"Yeah," Garrett said. "Me too."

"Are you going to call the police?" Ernie asked.

Mrs. Price shook her head. "And say what? That you saw a ghost with a spear?"

"Yes!" we shouted.

"I tell you what," Mr. Price said. "Let me just take a flashlight and check things out. Then we'll decide if we need to call anyone."

"No, Daddy!" Ellie cried. "Don't go out there by yourself!"

"Good point. Maybe I'll grab Ed to go with me."

"No!" the twins said.

"Don't tell me you still think Ed's a bad guy," he said.

"We don't know who the bad guy is anymore," I answered for everyone.

"Well, I can assure you it isn't Ed," Mr. Price said. "Look, I'll just make a quick run through the churchyard and be right back. Won't take but a minute."

"Be careful, Daddy," Ellie said, whimpering.

"Don't worry, sweetheart, I will."

While we waited for him to return, Mrs. Price took us all to the kitchen for milk and cookies. The cookies smelled delicious—still warm from the oven—but I munched on a carrot instead.

After only a few minutes, the front door slammed. "Well, I found something," Mr. Price announced from the foyer.

Ellie was up before I set my glass down. "You did?" she asked, almost running into her dad as he entered the kitchen.

"Yep. This." He threw the grocery bag of crumpled snacks on the table and sat down. "Listen, kids, I think you're letting this whole ghost thing get out of hand. Having a good imagination is one thing, but allowing it to take over your life is another." He put his hand on Garrett's shoulder but spoke to all of us. "Didn't your mom say to forget about all this ghost stuff?"

I wanted to ask him how we were supposed to do that with everything that was going on, but I didn't.

"Look," Mr. Price continued, "we'll keep an eye out, but the five of you need to concentrate on other things. And whatever you do, don't go looking for trouble."

CHAPTER · 16

ELLIE WANTED TO SLEEP LATE THE NEXT MORNING, BUT I couldn't waste the time. I climbed out of bed, grabbed the phone book, and threw it onto her bed. "What did you say that jeweler's name was—the one from your church? I need his phone number."

Ellie rubbed her eyes and yawned. "What's the rush? We haven't even had breakfast yet."

"The rush is that the week is almost over, and I still don't have enough money for camp. And now that I can't sell my jewelry at church, I'm going to have to go to Plan B. Maybe that man at church would sell Bitsy's Bangles in his store."

"Uh, I don't know. I don't think he handles your kind of jewelry."

"What's that mean? My stuff's not good enough?"

"No, it's not that." She hesitated. "It's just that he deals in real diamonds and emeralds, and real gold. Not fake stuff."

I jumped from the bed. "Fake? You call my stuff fake? Well, you sure were quick to take it when you got it for free!"

Ellie tried to make up with me. "Come on, Bitsy. It's just that he's used to dealing with grown-up jewelry. Yours is for kids."

I plopped down and pulled the phone book onto my lap. "Forget it, I'll find it myself."

Since I didn't have any idea about the name of the store, I decided to read the phone book, beginning with the A's. There sure were a lot of businesses named Amelia Island this and Amelia Island that. Nothing as creative as Bitsy's Bangles.

I ran my finger down the page . . . and stopped. My heart jumped into my throat. "Ellie, you're not going to believe this."

She sat up and read over my shoulder. "Amelia Island Ghost Tours? What could that mean?"

"What do you think it means?" I said. "It means there really are ghosts on Amelia Island, and now we can find out the truth about them."

Garrett and I banged on the twins' front door before Ellie reached their bottom step.

"Be there in a minute," Ernie yelled from inside.

I sat on the porch and ran my fingers through my hair, still damp from the latest dose of Sun-Glow. Things were looking better. The swelling in my right eye was completely gone, my scabs were a little smaller, and my hair was definitely changing color. I sure would be glad when it was completely blonde.

All it had taken was a phone call to the twins to get things going. Ellie and Bernie weren't sure we needed to investigate this newest finding, but the boys saw things my way.

"Come on," I said once everybody was outside. "I want to check something out before we head to the store."

"What now?" Ellie whined.

I walked toward the cemetery. "I just want to look over the cemetery one more time."

"Bitsy, Daddy checked it out last night," she said. "We don't need to go back again."

"Yeah, but it was dark then. It'll be easier to see now."

"Come on, Ellie," Garrett said. "It's not a big deal."

She squinted at her brother. "You're not the boss of me."

"Quit arguing and come on," I said, leading the way. I didn't think it was such a big deal, either. The church, the trees, the monument, the cemetery—they all looked very innocent in the daylight. Mrs. Price was probably right. There had to be a simple explanation for what we'd seen.

"Okay," I said. "Everybody spread out and look carefully."

"What are we looking for?" Bernie asked.

"I don't know. Anything that seems suspicious, I guess. Anything that doesn't look like it belongs."

Garrett came out from behind the magnolia tree. "You mean something like this?" He waved the evidence in his hand.

We ran to him and I grabbed it. "What is it?" Ellie asked.

I held up the white cloth. "I'm not sure what it is, but look—it belongs to someone with the initials S. O."

"What?" Ernie jerked the clue from me and studied it. "I think it's a handkerchief. Either that or a diaper."

"Don't be silly," I said, taking back the cloth. "Babies don't have monogrammed diapers. And I should know—we've had enough diapers at my house." Then I stuffed it in my pocket. "Come on. We can talk about it on the way to the grocery store."

We started back down the sidewalk when Ernie said, "You never did explain what the grocery store had to do with the ghosts."

"It's simple. When I called the number for Amelia Island Ghost Tours, there was a recording that said the tours start at Shorty's every Friday night at eight o'clock."

"But today's Thursday," Ellie said.

"So? There's no reason we can't ask Mr. Shorty about ghosts today." Then it hit me. "Oh, man!" I grabbed my head and walked round and round in circles. "Oh, man!"

"What?" Garrett asked.

"What?" Ernie said louder.

I pulled the white material from my pocket and considered the initials again. "What's Mr. Shorty's last name?"

Garrett rubbed his chin. "Uh, Shorty . . . Shorty. . . ." His mouth dropped open, and he jerked the cloth from my hand. "Owens!"

"Let's go!" I yelled.

"Wait," Garrett said. "We've got to have a plan. We can't just go barging in there and accuse Mr. Shorty of trying to steal something, and then say we know he's trying to scare us with ghosts."

I stared at Garrett. "Why not? It's the truth."

"Yeah, but—"

"We'll just ask him questions and see how he answers them," I said. "That'll tell us a lot. And watch his eyes. The eyes are the windows to the soul."

Ernie raised his eyebrows. "The windows to the soul?" He laughed. "Where'd you get that?"

Garrett laughed and high-fived Ernie.

"I don't know," I replied. "I read it somewhere. Look, that's not important. Just do what I said—watch and listen."

CHAPTER · 17

BY THE TIME WE REACHED SHORTY'S, I COULD TELL THAT I was going to have to lead this investigation. I took the clue from my pocket and walked right up to Mr. Shorty. "Is this yours?"

"Good morning to you, too," Mr. Shorty said.

I didn't say anything.

He took the evidence from my hands. "Mine? Why would you think it's mine?"

Aha! He answered a question with a question—a true sign of guilt! "Well, because it has your initials on it."

"My initials?"

Aha! Another question—guilty for sure! I hoped the others were paying attention. "Yes, sir. Right here, in the corner. S. O. Shorty Owens."

Then he laughed, a big laugh that made his belly jiggle. I just stood there. I didn't see anything funny.

He wiped his eyes. "Whoever heard of parents naming their kid Shorty?" He pulled a handkerchief from his pocket and blew his nose. I couldn't tell if it had any initials monogrammed on it or not. "My name's Alvin. Alvin Owens. Everybody just calls me Shorty. It's a nickname. You know, sorta like Bitsy."

He held out the clue and said, "Hey, now that you know my real name, don't you think you ought to tell me yours?"

I grabbed the cloth and stomped out the door. No way was I going to tell him my name. After all, Elizabeth Ruth Burroughs wasn't the one on trial here. He was.

My friends followed me outside, and Garrett said, "What do you think? Is he guilty?"

"Tell us," Bernie begged.

I crossed my arms. "I don't know. But he's hiding something—I'm sure of that. We need to ask him some more questions. Come on, and pay attention."

I led the way back into the store, where Mr. Shorty was loading a lady's groceries.

The lady was talking. "I think we ought to forget about a resource center myself. What if the house really is haunted?"

I motioned for the gang to follow me behind a rack of magazines.

"I don't know, Sarah," Mr. Shorty said. "I think everybody's getting all worked up over nothing."

The lady continued. "Well, you have to admit, Hawkins was always weird. I mean, think about it—

you were his own flesh and blood, and he wouldn't even speak to you. It'd be just like him to come back and haunt us."

"I guess everybody's entitled to their own opinion, but I'd hate to see us lose the chance for a resource center. People like Ricky could sure use it." Mr. Shorty put the last of the lady's groceries in the cart. "That should do it, Sarah. Hope you have a good week. Oh, here's Ricky now. He'll be glad to get that for you."

A man in white coveralls walked up to the cart. He seemed a little familiar, and then I remembered he was one of the men I'd bumped into at the open house. He spoke to the lady. "Hey, Miz Hubbard. How's Justin doin'?"

"He's doing great, Ricky. How kind of you to ask."

Ricky grinned and lowered his head. Then he just started laughing, for no reason at all. The lady laughed, too, and Ricky pushed the groceries out the door.

I started out from behind the magazines and then saw another man I remembered from the open house.

He glanced around the store before speaking. "So, Shorty, did you find out anything about the missing picture?"

Garrett grabbed Ernie's shirtsleeve. "We forgot about the picture," he whispered. "Do you have it?"

Ernie shook his head. "We searched our house but couldn't find it."

"What did your aunt say?"

"We didn't get to ask her. We were asleep by the time she got home from work, and she'd already left when we got up this morning. I don't know where that picture is, but I can tell you this—it's not in our house."

We all got quiet and turned our attention back to the men.

"Nope," Mr. Shorty said, "I haven't found out a thing, Norman. But I still can't believe you'd bid on that picture for me. Nobody's ever been so nice to me in my whole life."

So, this was Norman—the man Mr. Shorty had talked to the day before about the picture—and the same man who was at the open house!

"Don't mention it," Mr. Norman said.

"Why are you kids hiding behind the magazines?"

We nearly broke our necks turning around to see who'd caught us. It was Mr. Ed.

"Seen any ghosts lately?" Then he winked and walked toward the other men. "Hey, Shorty."

We leaned around the stand to watch.

"Good morning, Ed," Mr. Shorty said. "Have you met my good friend Norman?"

"I don't think we've met officially, but I remember seeing you at the open house the other night. You planning on bidding at the auction?"

"I think so." Mr. Norman smiled at Mr. Shorty. "There are a few items I'm interested in."

Garrett jabbed me with his elbow. "Did you hear that?"

"Ouch!" I yelled.

The men turned in our direction, and Mr. Ed spoke up. "Let me introduce you to my noisy friends here. Come on over, kids."

We came out from behind the magazine stand and ambled over to Mr. Ed.

"This is Garrett and Ellie Price," he said. "They live in the Nuns' House . . . you know, where we had the open house."

"Oh, yes," Mr. Norman said.

Then Mr. Ed pointed to the twins. "This is Ernie and Bernie. They live beside me, across from the Prices."

Everybody smiled at everybody.

Then Mr. Ed nodded at me. "And this is Bitsy. She's visiting from South Carolina."

Mr. Shorty smiled. "Yes, Bitsy and I have met."

"Really? I didn't realize you two knew each other."

"Oh, Bitsy and I go way back. We're old friends, aren't we, kiddo?" Mr. Shorty muffled a laugh.

I didn't smile.

Mr. Ed started up again. "The kids have been doing some investigating lately, and . . ."

What is he doing? I wondered. I shook my head at Mr. Ed, but he didn't get the message.

". . . it seems they've had a run-in with a ghost."

Is he making fun of us?

Mr. Shorty started laughing again, out loud this time.

That made me mad. "We *did* see a ghost! Two, to be exact."

Mr. Ed didn't laugh. "Two?"

"Yes, sir. The one at Mr. Hawkins's house, and then another one at the cemetery last night."

"The cemetery?" Mr. Ed said. "I didn't know about that one."

I pulled the white clue out of my pocket. "That's where we found this."

"So that's why you were grilling me about that bandana, huh?" Mr. Shorty said. "You think I have something to do with your ghost?"

Garrett jumped into the conversation. "It's not *our* ghost. We don't want a ghost. We just want some answers. That's why we came to see you."

"Me?" Mr. Shorty said. "Why me?"

"Because of that white thing we found with your initials on it," Garrett said, "and the fact that you run the ghost tours."

"Whoa! Wait a minute," Mr. Shorty said. "I can see where you might think that bandana's mine, but what's this about ghost tours?"

I decided to answer that one. "When I called the phone number to find out about the ghost tours, the recording said to meet in your parking lot at eight o'clock on Friday nights."

Mr. Shorty didn't laugh this time. "I guess it does look kind of suspicious."

We had him! "Yes, sir, it does."

"Only problem is, it's not my bandana, and I don't have anything to do with the ghost tours. They just like to meet in my parking lot since most of the haunted houses are in this area."

My heart felt like a jackhammer pounding in my chest. I waited for my friends to say something, but no one moved a muscle. "Haunted houses?" I said. "So there really are haunted houses on Amelia Island?"

"Sure!" Mr. Shorty said. "Why else would they have ghost tours?"

"Now, wait a minute, Shorty," Mr. Ed said.

But I couldn't wait. "Do you know if the Pogy Witch Woman is true?"

"Oh, yeah," Mr. Shorty said. "She's been around for a long time." Then he leaned down to our level. "If you see a light come on in the woods, you'd better get out of there—she's coming after you!"

Mr. Ed stepped between Mr. Shorty and us. "Okay, okay. That's enough. Kids, don't pay any attention to Shorty. He's just pulling your leg."

We all looked at Mr. Shorty. He grinned.

"Well, I believe in ghosts," a voice said behind us. We turned to see a woman with a cart half full of groceries. "I think it's absurd that the town would even consider taking that house, knowing it's haunted. And I'll tell you something else—you won't find me bidding on anything. They're not getting a cent of my money." She pushed her cart toward the next aisle. "And I'm not the only one in town who feels this way, either."

Mr. Ed shook his head. "Listen, kids, I was in the police business for a long time, and I'm telling you, you're better off dealing with facts, not folktales. And that's all these ghost stories are—folktales. Now, why don't y'all just forget about all this and go on home?"

"But—" Garrett started.

"No buts," Mr. Ed said.

We just stood there a second, then Mr. Ed nodded toward the door. Nobody said a word as we left the store and walked across the parking lot. Finally, I couldn't take it any longer. I dropped down to the sidewalk and leaned against the fence. My friends lined up beside me.

"Mr. Ed says we need to deal with facts," I said. "So let's do it. What are the facts? Do those ghosts really exist?"

A deep voice answered behind us. "Personally, I think they do."

Ellie screamed. We looked up to see Mr. Norman—Mr. Shorty's friend—the man who was visiting from St. Augustine.

"You . . . you do?" I asked.

"Sure. I've seen them myself." He unwrapped a piece of Teaberry gum.

Garrett stood. "You've seen the ghosts? You've seen the ghosts on Amelia Island?"

"Yeah, plenty of times." He put the gum in his mouth and threw the paper on the ground. "Lots of them," he whispered. "Even saw one at Hawkins's house once. It was really scary."

"Have you seen the Pogy Witch Woman?" Ernie asked.

The man rubbed his chin and slowly nodded his head. "As a matter of fact, I have."

Ernie jumped up. "Mr. Ed says we need to deal with facts. As much as I hate to say it, maybe we do need to go to the Pogy Plant tonight. Then we can prove if she's real or not."

"I don't know, kids," Mr. Norman said. "You know what Ed said."

"Yes, sir," Ernie said, "but remember what he said about facts. What better way to get the facts than to find out for ourselves?"

"Whatever," the man said. "But be careful. I'd hate for anything to happen to you."

We watched as he limped back toward the parking lot. Without a word, we all took off running back to the yellow house. We had plans to make.

CHAPTER · 18

WE CAMPED OUT ON GARRETT'S BED, TRYING TO MAKE some sense of everything we knew so far.

"Okay, we know that Mr. Shorty fits the profile," I started as I wrote his name at the top of the page.

"The profile?" Garrett said. "I think you've been watching too much TV. Are you trying to sound like a detective or something?"

"Very funny. For your information, this is how it's done in real life. This is how they figure out mysteries."

Bernie scooted closer and rubbed her fingers across my neck. "What's that?" she asked.

"What's what?"

"This mark on your neck. Looks like dirt."

Garrett leaned in. "Sure does. Did you take a bath this morning?"

"Of course I did. And why is everyone so interested in my neck all of a sudden?"

Ellie touched my arm. "Because it's dirty, Bitsy."

I threw down the paper and pen, jumped from the bed, and stomped toward the mirror. Even after three days, I was still shocked every time I saw my battered reflection looking back at me. But this time there was a new problem—my neck really was dirty.

I ran to the bathroom and grabbed a clean washcloth, lathered it up with soap, and started scrubbing. My friends crowded around me.

"Is it coming off?" Ellie asked.

"Of course it's coming off. What did you expect?"

"I guess I didn't expect it to be dirty." She reached for my necklace. "Here, let me get this so you can get it all off." Ellie unclasped the hook and removed my Bitsy's Bangle. The gold "B" dangled from her fingers.

Bernie put in her two cents worth. "Aunt Myrna says we have to take a bath every day, whether we need one or not."

"I do take a bath every day. I told you that."

Ernie spoke up. "Well, looks like you missed a spot." He nudged Garrett and smiled.

Garrett smiled back. I wasn't sure this new friendship was working out so great after all. I mean, since when did Garrett take sides against me?

I inspected the soapy washcloth but didn't see any dirt. I rinsed the cloth and wiped my neck again, removing all the lather. Then I studied my reflection. It was still there. "What's going on?" I yelled at the mirror.

Garrett draped his arm across my shoulders. "I hate to tell you, but I think maybe you're morphing into another species or something." He wasn't smiling.

That was the last straw. I brushed his arm off my shoulders, threw the washcloth into the sink, and dashed out of the room.

I found Mrs. Price in the kitchen with slices of jelly-covered bread lined up on the counter. "Y'all about ready for lunch?" she asked as I tromped into the room.

"No, ma'am," I answered. "I can't think of eating at a time like this."

She turned from the half-made sandwiches. "A time like what?"

"A time like *this.*" I pointed to my neck.

Garrett's mom leaned over and studied the defect. "Hmm. Looks like dirt to me. Did you take a bath this morning?"

My so-called friends laughed.

"I did, I promise." I rubbed my neck. "I don't think it's dirt. It won't come off, even with soap and water."

Mrs. Price leaned in closer, touched my left earlobe, and then inspected the right. "You know, now that you mention it, it looks like there's something on your ears, too."

"Oh no!" I yelled. "Whatever it is, it's spreading!"

Garrett grinned. "Hey, she really *is* morphing into another species!" He high-fived Ernie and then reached for the girls, but they ignored him.

Ellie put her arm around me. "It's okay, Bitsy. We'll figure out what's going on."

"Boys, nobody's morphing into anything," Mrs. Price said. "I'm sure there's a good explanation for this." She touched my neck again. "Have you done anything different since you've been here? Worn any new clothes? New perfume? I don't think it's the soap, because it's only right here."

"Well, I can't remember the last time I had new clothes, and I can assure you I'm not wearing any perfume, so that's not it."

Ellie snapped her fingers. "Your jewelry!"

"No," I answered, "I've worn that jewelry all year and haven't had a problem with it."

Mrs. Price rubbed her forehead. "Bitsy, I'm afraid Ellie's right. I'm afraid it *is* your jewelry."

"But it can't be! Like I said, I've worn it forever without any problem."

"But you haven't worn it at the beach. Things are different here. The salt in the air—and the humidity—can change the chemicals in your skin and cause jewelry to turn green. I'm afraid Bitsy's Bangles may be the culprit."

Then reality hit me. "Oh, no! What about everyone else? What about all my customers?"

"Maybe it's just because your skin isn't used to the air here. Maybe it won't bother anyone else." Mrs. Price paused. "I guess we'll just have to wait and see."

"Yeah, we'll have to wait and see if this is the beginning of the end for my business." I plopped down into a kitchen chair. "Grief!"

After lunch, we trooped upstairs and went back to work on our ghost investigation. But every few minutes, Ellie quietly slipped off the bed and went into the bathroom. She didn't say anything, but I knew she was checking her own neck. After about the tenth time, I said, "Why don't you just go ahead and take off your necklace? Then you won't have to worry about it anymore."

"You wouldn't mind? You wouldn't be mad at me?"

"No, I wouldn't be mad. Besides, you're driving me crazy getting up and down all the time."

Without saying a word, she left the room and returned without her Bitsy's Bangle. That was when I realized I was doomed to financial ruin.

CHAPTER · 19

WE ARGUED ALL AFTERNOON ABOUT WHETHER OR NOT to go to the Pogy Plant and check out the Witch Woman. Garrett, Ernie, and I wanted to find her. But Ellie and Bernie wouldn't budge, so we finally agreed we'd try to forget about all this mysterious stuff. Besides, between the talent show, my injuries, my dirty neck, and my failing business, I had enough to worry about without adding a ghost and a witch to the mess.

The problem was, the only night we could get free ice cream from Mr. Ed was also the night Mr. Price met with his friends at the Pogy Plant. We decided to take the Uno cards to keep us busy.

When the time came to go, we girls squeezed into the truck's tiny backseat and the guys climbed in the front with Mr. Price. Everybody was quiet, so my mind began to wander to all my problems . . . and the fact that everything boiled down to money. If my family had enough money, I wouldn't be worried about the talent show or camp or Bitsy's Bangles. The Prices sure seemed to have enough. I wondered where all their money came from.

After a few minutes, I spoke up. "Can I ask you something, Mr. Price?"

"Sure, Bitsy. What?"

"What do you pray for at this meeting—money?"

He laughed. "Well, all of us could use a little more of it, of course, but that's not what we pray for. We pray for our families, for the kids' schools, our jobs, our churches. We pray for other people and their needs. You know—the really important things in life."

"But isn't money really important?"

He tilted the rearview mirror so we could see each other. "Well, it's true you have to have money, but most of us put too much emphasis on it. I have to admit, I'm as guilty as anyone."

I sat in the backseat and considered what Mr. Price said. I knew I thought about money a lot, but it's hard not to think about it when you don't have enough of it. And the way things were going, I wasn't going to have enough for camp . . . or anything else, for that matter.

After a few minutes, Ellie's dad drove through the Pogy Plant gate and parked beside an old brick building. Turning off the ignition, he faced us and repeated his instructions. "Now, I'm serious—don't get in the water, don't try to get on the tugboat, and stay away from the crane."

"We won't, we won't, and we will," Garrett said.

Mr. Price smiled and tousled his son's hair. "I won't be long," he said. Then he climbed out and headed toward the building, where two men greeted him halfway.

"Who are they?" Ernie asked as we got out of the truck.

"The tall one is Mr. Johnny," Garrett answered. "This is his building here. He makes sport nets—like the backstops in baseball and the goals on soccer fields. And that other man is Mr. Bill. He owns the crane business over there."

We rounded the corner of the building. "And who owns that?" I pointed to a dilapidated, rusted tugboat at the edge of the water.

The guys and I took off toward the boat.

"Don't!" Ellie yelled. "We promised Daddy that we wouldn't get on it!"

"We're not getting on," I yelled. "We just want a closer look." With all the broken glass, trash, and engine parts scattered all over the place, I was glad I'd worn tennis shoes instead of sandals. When we got to the water's edge, I could see that the boat was chained to a metal post sticking up out of the ground. "So, whose is it?"

"I don't know," Garrett replied. "It's been sitting there for as long as we've been coming around."

"Wouldn't it be great to live on a houseboat?" Ernie said.

That sounded good to me. "Sure would. No bratty

sisters to bug me, no bawling baby brother to keep me awake."

"Quit dreaming and come on," Garrett said, slapping at his arm. "These mosquitoes are eating me alive down here by the water."

We started back toward the truck and stopped to gaze up at a crane stretched out in front of us. "What about that big thing?" I asked. "Is it always here?"

"No," Garrett said, "sometimes it's here and sometimes it's out on a job."

I started back up the slight incline, carefully stepping over the trash and junk. "You'd think these litterbugs could at least put their gum wrappers in their pockets, wouldn't you? I mean, how much trouble is that?"

Cre-a-k!

We stopped and spun around in time to see the tugboat bounce in the rippling water.

"Did you see that?" Ernie asked.

Ellie buried her head in my arm.

"Yeah," Garrett said, his voice cracking. "It . . . it must be a little wave coming in."

I looked out across the river but didn't see any boats. "Maybe it's the wind."

"Yeah, that's it," Bernie said. "The wind."

Ellie kept her head buried in my arm. "Can we just go now . . . please?" We turned again and headed back up the path. "I want to go inside," she said.

"You know we can't interrupt Daddy," Garrett said.

"Come on." He led the way to the truck, grabbed the Uno cards from the cab, and motioned for us to climb into the truck bed.

Ellie seemed to feel better after she won the first two hands of Uno, but before long, it was getting too dark to see the cards.

"Guess we'll have to go inside now," Garrett said.

Ellie stood. "Well, I'm ready!"

"Me, too," the twins answered together.

We climbed down from the truck, and Garrett opened the door to put the cards back inside the cab. I glanced out across the woods beside the building, then stared . . . and screamed. There, bouncing through the woods, was a bright, yellow light!

"The Pogy Witch Woman!" I yelled as I took off running.

Within seconds, we were a choir of screams rushing toward the old brick building. The men ran out to us and, without slowing down, dragged us—still screaming—inside.

"The Pogy Witch Woman!" Garrett yelled.

"We saw her! We saw her!" I screeched.

Ellie hugged her daddy, while Ernie and Bernie held on to the other men and cried. Garrett and I clung to each other and cried, too.

"Okay, everybody calm down," Mr. Price said. He grabbed Garrett by the shoulders. "Tell me what happened."

My friend wiped the tears from his eyes. "We saw her, Daddy. We saw the witch!"

His daddy looked over our heads to the other two men, still holding on to the twins. I could tell he was worried. "You saw someone? Where?"

"In the woods," I said. "We saw her in the woods. Over there." I pointed toward the end of the building.

Mr. Price ran out the door.

"Daddy!" Ellie screamed. "Don't go!"

But he was already gone. Ellie, Garrett, and I held each other tight.

Within a couple of minutes, Mr. Price was back inside. "Kids, come over here and sit down."

We gathered in a group of orange plastic chairs in the corner.

"Okay, now tell me again what happened," he said. "Bitsy, you start."

"We were getting ready to come in, when I saw a light flickering out in the woods . . ."

Ellie and Bernie started crying again.

". . . so I screamed. Then everybody else saw it, too."

After a pause, Mr. Price said, "Wait a minute. I thought you saw a woman."

"Well, we didn't actually see her . . . we saw her light," I explained.

He sighed. The other men rubbed their foreheads.

"It was her, Daddy," Garrett said. "We know it was."

"How? How do you know it was her?"

"Because Mr. Shorty and Mr. Norman have both seen her," Ernie said. "They said if you see her light, she's coming to get you."

Garrett looked at Ernie. "I thought you said you'd seen her, too."

"Well. . . ."

"You've never seen her before, have you?" Garrett stood up. "You lied to us."

Ernie jumped from his chair and rushed over to Garrett, his fists clinched. Mr. Johnny grabbed Ernie by the arms.

"Hey, wait a minute, buddy," Mr. Johnny said.

"Everybody just sit and calm down," Mr. Price said. "Now, if I understand correctly, the only thing you saw was a light. That's all—a light. Right, Bitsy?"

"Yes, but—" I started.

"Wait a minute, let me finish. You saw a light, so you screamed, and that's how we ended up where we are. Nobody saw a person or a body or a witch. Right?"

"Yes, sir," I admitted.

Mr. Bill spoke up for the first time. "Well, sounds to me like a perfect case of mistaken identity."

"I agree," Mr. Price said.

"But what about the light?" Ernie asked. "Where did it come from?"

"It came from the artists' retreat. It's a cabin out in the woods." Mr. Price pointed toward the end of the building. "Over there."

I studied the dirty floor while he continued. "Writers and artists and musicians go there all the time to have peace and quiet while they work." He smiled at the other men. "Guess they didn't get too much peace and quiet tonight."

The men laughed.

"But, Daddy—" Ellie started.

"No more discussion," Mr. Price announced. "Time to get ice cream."

It took a few minutes, but we finally agreed we hadn't really seen anything mysterious after all. We piled back into the truck and headed to the ice cream shop.

"So, what flavor does everybody want?" Mr. Price asked.

I decided it was time to forget my healthy diet for a while and have a treat. "German chocolate cake."

"Vanilla," Garrett and Ellie said together.

"Rainbow," Ernie said.

Bernie rubbed her tummy. "Mmm. Bubble gum."

"Bubble gum?" Ellie said. "Yuck! I hope you don't expect me to lick it when it starts dripping."

"Of course not. I can do all the licking by myself."

We laughed. It was good to feel safe again.

As soon as Mr. Price parked, we jumped from the big truck and ran into the ice cream shop.

"Well, there you are," Mr. Ed said. "I was about to give up on you."

"Sorry," Mr. Price said. "We had a little delay at the Pogy Plant."

"Delay?"

"Oh, nothing," I said. "We thought we saw something out in the woods, but it was just someone at the artists' retreat."

"The artists' retreat?" Mr. Ed said. "No, I don't think anyone's out there this week. The whole thing's covered in black plastic while they treat it for termites. Now, what kind of ice cream did you kids want?"

Nobody answered. Ice cream didn't sound so good after all.

CHAPTER · 20

THE PHONE WOKE ME UP THE NEXT MORNING. I ROLLED over and tried to go back to sleep. But just about the time I dozed off, it rang again. I gave up and headed downstairs. It rang a third time as I entered the kitchen. Mrs. Price picked it up.

"No, she's not up yet. . . . Oh, I'm so sorry, Mallory. . . . Sure, I'll give Bitsy the message." Mrs. Price placed the phone back on the hook, saw me, and jumped. "Oh, you startled me, Bitsy."

"I'm sorry. Was that call for me?"

"Um-hum. It's the third one this morning."

"For me? Who'd be calling me?"

"Honey, it's what we were afraid of."

My heart started pounding. "They found the Pogy Witch Woman?"

Mrs. Price laughed. "No, no, not that. It's your jewelry."

This time I was sure my heart would stop beating

altogether. I dragged myself over to the kitchen table and pulled out a chair. "Grief!"

Mrs. Price and I sat at the table and counted my money. "Forty-five, fifty, fifty-five, sixty. I have sixty dollars," I said. "Now, how many want their money back?"

"*Double* their money back, remember?" she said.

I fell back against the chair and looked up at the ceiling. "Oh, my goodness, that means I have to give them each ten dollars! How many are there?"

"Let's see, you had three calls before you got up . . . and then three more since then."

"Sixty dollars!" I threw the money on the table. "That's all of it—gone."

Neither one of us said a word as the clock tick-tick-ticked on the wall.

"Pretty girl," Mooshew said.

I jumped when the phone rang. Mrs. Price answered it. "Hello."

"Hello, pretty girl," Mooshew said.

Mrs. Price continued. "Yes, she's here."

I frowned at Ellie's mom and shook my head back and forth.

"I'm sorry, but could I take a message? Yes, I'll tell her. She'll be back in touch." Ellie's mom hung up the phone, pulled her chair next to mine, and put her arm around me.

I leaned my head on her shoulder and cried.

* * *

Ellie and I stood at the mirror and brushed our teeth. My friend stopped and leaned against the counter. "So my mom's giving you the ten dollars you need to pay everybody back?"

I rinsed the toothbrush and put it back in the holder. "She's loaning it to me. I have to pay her back."

"How are you going to do that?"

"I'm not sure. Hey, what about that man from your church that owns the jewelry store?"

"Um, Bitsy, I don't think he's going to sell your jewelry. He doesn't want unhappy customers, either."

"I'm not talking about selling my jewelry. I was thinking maybe he'd let me work for him today and tomorrow—you know, to make a little money. I'm a good saleswoman."

"Bitsy, you're twelve years old."

"So?"

Ellie rolled her eyes. She was really getting good at doing that. "Well, at least your face is a little better. Maybe you could win the talent show, after all."

I turned to the mirror and studied my reflection. "Look. My hair. It's . . . it's different."

She covered her mouth and said, "Oh, my goodness. It *is* different."

I picked up the Sun-Glow and started spraying.

Ellie grabbed my arm. "What are you doing?"

"What do you think I'm doing? The Sun-Glow's

finally starting to work. I'm not going to stop now."

"But Bitsy, it's not blonde. It's . . . it's weird."

I set the bottle down hard on the counter. "It's not weird, it's auburn. And everybody knows auburn is a cool color."

That afternoon, Mr. Price came home from work early so he could help his wife get ready for the auction. "Hurry up, Garrett," he called from the kitchen. "I need you kids to help me with the chairs."

Ellie and I carried our glasses to the dishwasher.

Mrs. Price ran through the back door and plopped two bottles of cleaning solution and a handful of dirty rags on the kitchen counter. "There. I've finished wiping down the chairs. You guys can get them set up now. And hurry. A couple of people are already out there." She started back out the door.

Mr. Price grabbed his wife and hugged her. "Okay, now take two minutes to catch your breath."

"I don't have two minutes to catch my breath," she said, trying to free herself from his hold. But he wouldn't let go. "Okay, okay, I'll take a break," she said, laughing.

Mr. Price walked over to the sink, filled a glass with water, and pulled back the curtain. "I really thought there'd be more people there by now."

"Me, too," Mrs. Price said, taking the water. "Maybe they're just running late."

Mooshew flew overhead and landed on the table, right in front of Ellie's mom.

"Shoo!" she said. "Get back on your perch, Mooshew."

The pink cockatoo did as he was told and returned to his wooden perch.

That's one smart bird, I thought.

We heard a knock at the door. Ellie opened it and said, "Hey, Ricky. Come in."

He shuffled into the kitchen and grinned at Ellie's mom.

"Hello, Ricky," she said. "It's good to see you."

He lowered his head and laughed. "It's good to see you, too, Miz Price." He kept his eyes on the floor. "I came to see if I could help you with anything. I like to help people."

"Well, thank you, Ricky. That's very nice of you."

He shuffled his feet. "Oh, it weren't nothing."

Screech! Mooshew darted from his perch and soared overhead, zooming back and forth across the room.

"Mooshew, stop it!" Mrs. Price said. "Get in your cage right now." We watched as she shoved the bird in and closed the door. Mooshew paced. "And you're not coming back out, young man!"

Ricky ran to Mrs. Price. "Why did you do that? Why did you do that?" He rubbed his head and stepped from one foot to the other.

"What's the matter, Ricky? What did I do?"

Ricky whimpered and ran out the door.

Mrs. Price took off after him. "Ricky! Wait!"

The rest of us just stood in the middle of the kitchen.

"What was that all about?" Mr. Price said.

"I'm not sure," I said, "but I think Ricky was taking up for Mooshew."

CHAPTER · 21

AFTER LOSING ALL OF MY MONEY OVER THAT SILLY guarantee, I'd decided to change my line of business, and my friends were going to help. Even Mrs. Price agreed to loan me a little more money if I needed it to get started. We finished setting up the chairs and hurried to scout out the loot, looking for any old jewelry I could buy and resell. Since I wouldn't have to offer a guarantee for this old stuff, I figured I'd do pretty good with Bitsy's Bargains.

"Hi, guys."

We looked up to see the twins walking across the yard.

"Today's the big day, huh?" Ernie said when he reached us.

Ellie left my side and ran to Bernie. I tried not to let it hurt my feelings.

"Yep," Garrett answered. "My mom's sure hoping to bring in lots of money for the resource center."

I threw a broken necklace back in its box. "Money. Everything's always about money, isn't it?"

Nobody answered.

"Don't you agree?" I said.

Everybody just glared at me.

"What?"

Ellie curled a lock of straw-colored hair behind her ear. "Didn't you hear anything my dad said last night?"

"Huh?"

The gang studied their feet. Garrett finally spoke up. "You have to admit, Bitsy, you do think about money a lot."

"I think about it a lot 'cause I don't have it. You don't know what it's like, Garrett. *You* get to go to movies and have cool clothes. Your family has plenty of money."

"I know what it's like," Bernie said softly.

Nobody said anything.

She continued. "But I've realized these past few days that money isn't all that important, as long as you have people who love you. And, Bitsy, you have lots of people who love you."

I ran my fingers through my auburn hair and thought of Daddy and Mother and my little sisters and brother back home. I thought of Mr. and Mrs. Price and Garrett and Ellie and Nicolas. I thought of Ernie and Bernie and Mr. Ed. I thought of my church at home and Mr. and Mrs. Lyles at church here. Bernie was right. I had lots of people who loved me, whether I had any money or not.

The garbled voice of the auctioneer echoed over the sound system as we rummaged through boxes of old comic books.

"I know I can't bid on it," said a voice behind us, "but I'd still like to know where it is."

Then we heard Mr. Ed. "So, you're telling the truth, Shorty? You really don't have that picture?"

"Of course I don't. I'd never steal it, even though I do deserve it more than anybody else."

Ernie jumped up and took in a big breath. "The box!" he whispered. "Aunt Myrna remembered she had it in the back of her car and said for me to bring it over this morning. Run tell your mom—I'll go get it and be right back!"

He took off, and the rest of us searched for Mrs. Price. We found her inside Mr. Hawkins's house, grabbing another box to put on the auction block.

She was glad to hear our story. "Oh, good. Maybe there'll be something in there somebody'll bid on. They sure aren't bidding much on what we've put out so far."

Ernie ran up with the box, the family portrait visible over the edge. He handed the box to Mrs. Price. "Aunt Myrna said to tell you she's sorry. She forgot she still had it." Then he cleared his throat. "And I'm sorry we took it in the first place."

"That's okay, Ernie. At least we have it now," she said, carrying it out the door.

We followed her outside and watched as she whispered something to the auctioneer.

"Ladies and gentlemen, I have an announcement," he said. "I've just been informed that a new box of merchandise has been discovered. We'll place it up here for your examination, and it'll be auctioned in ten minutes."

I watched out of the corner of my eye as Mr. Norman hobbled to the front. Without touching a thing, he leaned over, glanced into the box, turned around, and smiled. I followed his gaze—straight to Mr. Shorty, who smiled back.

I took off running. "Come on!" I called to my friends. When we reached the Prices' kitchen, I filled them in on what I'd seen. "So now we know for sure the people on the monitor were looking for this picture. And they were talking about haunting Mr. Hawkins's house, not ours."

Ernie rubbed his forehead. "So that means Mr. Shorty was one of the men talking on the monitor the other night. Now, if we only knew who the other one was."

Garrett opened the refrigerator and grabbed bottles of water. "But I always thought Mr. Shorty was a nice guy."

"He is, normally," Ellie said, taking her water. "He

just wants that picture that has his mom it it. I can understand that. I think he should have it, too."

I plopped down in a chair. "But don't you think he was getting a little worked up over a family picture? He told Mr. Ed he was so mad he could choke somebody, and on the monitor, he talked about sending a ghost to scare people. I mean, I love my family and all, but it sounds a little extreme to me."

Bernie took a drink and headed back toward the door. "Come on. Let's get back out there and see what happens."

We searched the small crowd until we found Mr. Shorty and Mr. Norman huddled behind a huge yucca plant. We snuck around to the other side and pretended to wait for the bidding to start.

"Thanks again for doing this," Mr. Shorty said.

"Don't mention it," Mr. Norman answered.

"Hey, you know, I think I remember the lawyer saying someone named Bridges was interested in buying some things in the house. Was that you?"

"Me? No, I've never been here before. I'm just in town for the auction."

The microphone crackled as the auctioneer prepared to restart the bidding. He walked over to Ernie's box and carried it to the table. "Okay, let's see what we have here." He pulled out a vase, a matching set of candlesticks . . . and the picture. "Who'll open the bidding at ten dollars?"

Mr. Norman barely nodded his head.

"Ten dollars! We have ten dollars! Who'll go twenty?" He pointed to the other side of the little crowd. "We have twenty dollars! Now, who'll go thirty? Only thirty dollars for this great collection!"

A minute later, Mr. Norman walked to the front to get his prize. He forked over thirty dollars, picked up the box, and left.

Then I watched Mr. Shorty stuff his hands into his pockets and nod at Mr. Ed. Too bad Mr. Ed didn't know who the box really belonged to. Without a word, I left the group and followed Mr. Norman to the side yard.

Before he got very far, Ricky came bounding around the opposite corner of the house. "Mr. Norman!" he yelled, waving his arms in the air. Ricky joined the older man. "I'm glad they found it. I wanted you to get it."

Mr. Norman never looked up as he hobbled on his way. "Whatever," he said, leaving the young man alone in the street.

Ricky slumped and dropped his head as he shuffled toward me.

I walked over to him. "Don't pay any attention to Mr. Norman. He's just not very nice."

Putting his hand up to his mouth, Ricky leaned over and whispered in my ear, "Don't mention it."

Walking back to the house, I decided none of it was

really a big deal after all. I mean, everything came out okay. Mr. Shorty had the picture of his mother he wanted, Mr. Norman got to do something nice for someone, and the charity had another thirty dollars for the resource center. Obviously, Ricky was okay with it.

But if everything was going so good, why was I still feeling so bad?

I got back to the group in time to see my friends taking down the chairs.

"Where've you been?" Garrett yelled. "Can't you see all the work we've still got to do?"

I reached for a chair and started folding.

"Hey, kids!" It was Mr. Shorty. "Have y'all seen Norman? Norman Bridges?"

"No, sir," the others answered.

I spoke up. "I saw him leave."

"When? When did he leave?"

"A few minutes ago. Right after he bought the box with your picture in—" I realized what I was saying as soon as I saw his eyes 'bout pop out of his head.

"That double-crossing. . . ," Mr. Shorty mumbled as he took off toward the street.

"Way to go," Ernie said. "Now he knows we know about the picture."

"It's no big deal," I said with more enthusiasm than I felt. "I agree with Ellie—he deserves that family portrait."

"Yeah," Ernie said, "but I'm beginning to think there's more to it than meets the eye.

Garrett picked up another chair. "Great. Now *you're* the one sounding like a TV detective. I guess you've been around Bitsy too long."

"Very funny," I said. "Very funny."

CHAPTER · 22

THE COMMITTEE MEMBERS WERE ALL GATHERED around the Prices' kitchen table, while my friends and I sat on the floor.

Mrs. Price flipped through a stack of money. "Two hundred and twenty-six dollars. I can't believe the auction didn't bring in any more than this. Hardly anybody came, and most of the ones who did come didn't buy anything."

"Well," I said, "it would've worked out great if everybody hadn't been so upset about the ghost."

All the adults frowned at me. That's when I realized maybe this wasn't the best time to bring it up.

"What ghost?" an older man asked.

Mr. Price answered for me. "It seems the kids thought they saw a ghost in Hawkins's house earlier this week." He gave us an accusing look. "Guess it kind of leaked out."

Garrett jumped up. "But we didn't tell a soul!"

We all tried to talk at once, but before we could get it out, Mr. Ed came in the back door. "Did someone mention a ghost?" He threw a DVD case on the table. "Found this in one of the boxes I bought at the auction."

Mrs. Price picked up the case and read aloud, "A collection of ghosts, goblins, and ghouls."

Mr. Ed took off his green ball cap and scratched his head. "It's a visual-effects collection from the library, but Hawkins didn't have a DVD player. As a matter of fact, he only had a black-and-white TV." He pulled out a chair and sat down. "Looks like someone else had it in the house."

Garrett said, "Hey, what if someone was trying to scare us, so they projected a DVD of a ghost on the wall?"

Mr. Ed rubbed his chin. "Yeah, they could use a battery backup to do it."

"Or what if they were trying to scare us"—Mr. Price opened his arms to those at the table—"the committee, the town council, the families on the island. What if this person didn't want the auction to be successful?"

"But why would anybody do that?" Mr. Ed asked. "The resource center is a great idea, one that will help the entire community."

I couldn't keep my mouth shut any longer. "What if this person was only concerned about himself and what he wanted?"

Boy, did that open a can of worms. The adults suddenly became real interested in what we had to say, so we told everybody about everything—the conversation we heard over the monitor, the ghost at Mr. Hawkins's house and the one at the cemetery, and the Pogy Witch Woman. We even told them about the white bandana and what Mr. Shorty had said about ghosts. But everybody was shocked when we told them that Mr. Norman wasn't really interested in the picture at all, that he was only bidding on it for Mr. Shorty.

"Well," Mr. Price said, "I guess Shorty isn't concerned about anyone but himself. I just can't believe he'd try to scare everybody away from the resource center. I mean, you'd think he'd want it to work out for Ricky, if nothing else."

Mr. Ed pushed away from the table and stood. "You want me to talk to him?"

"Yeah," Ellie's dad said. "I'll go with you, since it looks like I've been on the fringe of it all." He kissed Mrs. Price on the cheek. "We'll be back as soon as we can." Stopping on the way to the door, he added, "You kids need to get to bed—especially you, Bitsy."

"Me?"

"Yes, you. Isn't the talent show tomorrow?"

I jumped up, my hand over my mouth. "The talent show! Oh, my goodness—I forgot all about that!" I ran out of the room and dashed up the stairs two at a time, laughter echoing up from the kitchen.

The boys went to Garrett's room to get ready for bed, while we girls headed into Ellie's. I pulled out the frilly dress, high heels, hose, feather boa, and pearls.

"Who's that for?" Bernie asked.

"Who do you think it's for?" I said. "Who's the only one around here brave enough to be in a talent show?"

"But it . . . it just doesn't look like you, Bitsy."

"I agree with you there." I threw myself on Ellie's bed and grabbed my head. "Oh, why am I doing this?"

Ellie sat down beside me. "Because you need the money, remember? You need that money for camp. And now you need even more money to pay my mom back."

Bernie stretched out beside me and stared up at the ceiling. "Sounds like you're going backwards to me. Sounds like you're just losing money."

"You're right, I am."

Ellie stood and grabbed my arm. "Well, whining about it certainly doesn't solve anything. Come on, let's see what we can do with your face." She pulled me out of bed.

"I don't whine," I said, as the three of us walked to the bathroom.

I sat on the toilet lid and let Ellie do something I thought I'd never let her do—put makeup on me. She tried every makeup trick she knew, but none of them did anything to cover the bruises, scrapes, and jewelry stain.

"To be honest," Bernie said, "I think it makes them show up more."

I agreed. "Besides, my elbows and knees are still going to show."

"Why don't you just forget it?" Bernie asked. "Who says you have to be in the show anyway?"

"My mother, for one. She paid the five-dollar entrance fee. She'd kill me if I backed out."

"Well, could you at least do something about your hair?"

I reached up and touched my curls. "My hair? What's wrong with my hair?"

"It's . . . I don't know. It's . . . orange."

"It's not orange, it's auburn," I said, jumping up from the toilet lid. I flipped on all the bathroom lights, leaned into the mirror . . . and thought I was going to throw up.

My hair was orange.

CHAPTER · 23

I WAS DREAMING I'D JUST HIT A HOME RUN AGAINST THE Mustangs when Mrs. Price shook me out of my sleep on Saturday morning. "Time to get up, girls. It's the Fourth of July."

"Don't remind me," I croaked.

"Well, I thought you might be interested in what we found out last night."

That did it. I sat up and rubbed my eyes.

"Shorty says he didn't have anything to do with the ghosts or the Pogy Plant and that it wasn't him on the monitor."

Ellie rolled over, her yellow bed-head sticking out against the pillow. "What'd he say about the picture?"

"He did admit that Norman was bidding on the picture for him, but he hasn't seen Norman since yesterday. Nobody has."

"Did he deny telling us about the ghosts and the Pogy Witch Woman?" Bernie asked.

"No, but he said he was only kidding. Said he was playing along since y'all were so serious about it."

There was a pause when no one said anything. I looked at Mrs. Price. She was studying my hair. "Umm, Bitsy—"

"I know. It's orange."

Ellie's mom shook her head, sat on the bed, and wrapped her arms around me. "Not having a very good week, are you?"

I took a big breath and sighed it back out. It felt good to be hugged. "Well, in some ways it's been a really good week. But I have a feeling the worst is yet to come."

The phone rang downstairs.

"Bitsy, it's for you," Mr. Price called.

"See what I mean? Grief!" I fell back against Ellie's mom. "Do you have another ten dollars I could borrow?"

She tousled my orange hair as I climbed over her legs.

Dragging myself into the kitchen, I heard Mr. Price talking on the phone. "Here she is." He handed me the phone.

He sure is being nice to someone who's about to take my money, I thought as I took the receiver from him. "Hello?"

"Hey, sugar."

"Daddy!" I suddenly felt much better.

"How are you this morning?"

"You don't want to know, Daddy."

"What? Are you okay, sweetheart?"

"No, sir, I'm not okay." Then it all tumbled out. "I have a black eye and bruises and scrapes all over my body, I have to sing a ridiculous song wearing ridiculous clothes while I act like a silly girly-girl, I have orange hair, my business is ruined, and I have no money for camp."

"Your business is ruined?" Leave it to Daddy to talk business.

I told him about my double-your-money-back guarantee and that it cost me everything, and more. "And now I owe Ellie's mom ten dollars. Where am I going to get ten dollars?"

"What about the talent show?"

"The talent show? Daddy, I can't win the talent show now. Who's going to believe I'm a prissy girl when I look like this? There's no need to even try . . . they'll just laugh at me."

"Bitsy, listen to me." Daddy was serious. "You're a good actress, and you know it."

"But Daddy—"

"Listen. A good actress can pretend to be anybody. You've said yourself that's the fun of acting—you can be someone else. So today, when you get on that stage, it won't be Bitsy dancing around up there, it'll be the prissiest girly-girl Amelia Island has ever seen!"

I started laughing.

"What?" Daddy asked. "What are you laughing about?"

"Daddy, you're a good actor, too. You sound like the President of the United States giving the State of the Union address. You should win an Oscar for your performance."

"Guess you get it honestly, huh?"

"Sure do," I said. "Okay, I'll give it a try."

"That's my girl."

"Oh, what about the letter from Channel Four? Did Mother get that appointment for me?"

"Well, sugar, I'm afraid that didn't work out, either."

"What?"

"They were looking for someone to sing on 'The Ben Leonard Show' at the last minute. They needed someone today."

"Grief!"

Chapter · 24

IT WAS FOUR O'CLOCK WHEN WE CLIMBED INTO MRS. Price's van. "Isn't this festival outside?" I asked.

Ellie's mom scanned the sky. "Yeah, it is. I sure hope this storm holds off long enough for the talent show."

"Not me. A big old storm with lots of lightning would be an answer to prayer right about now."

"Oh, Bitsy, you don't mean that. Come on, kids, buckle up. Ernie, you get up front with me since you're the biggest. The rest of you get in the back."

I held on to the van door and tried to hoist myself up. I lurched forward, fell over the middle seat, and twisted my ankle. "Man, I didn't realize it was so hard to walk in high-heeled shoes."

Mrs. Price snapped the buckle on Nicolas's car seat. "Haven't you ever walked in heels?" She got in the front seat and started the van.

"No, ma'am."

"And you didn't practice?"

"Um, no, ma'am. Guess I didn't think of that."

Garrett glanced over his shoulder. "Aren't you supposed to dance while you sing this prissy song?"

"Yeah, but not anything hard. It'll be okay." I reached up and repositioned my pearls to try to cover the jewelry stain on my neck.

Garrett shook his head and faced the front.

"Have they found Mr. Norman yet?" I asked Mrs. Price.

"No. I guess he knows his secret's out."

"Mom," Ellie called from the backseat, "where's the talent show going to be?"

"It's at Central Park, where we had Special Olympics last month. Remember?"

"Oh, yeah, that was so much fun." Ellie turned to me. "We helped give out the ribbons. Ricky was in it. He did good."

"He did do a good job," Mrs. Price said, "even though we couldn't convince him to race in running shorts and a T-shirt. Now that I think about it, I don't think I've ever seen him wearing anything but those white coveralls." She turned into the parking lot. "The pictures might still be up on the bulletin board in the alcove, Bitsy. Maybe you can see them while you wait to go onstage."

Mrs. Price parked the van, and we started piling out. I held on to the door and lowered myself to the ground, careful not to twist my ankle again.

"Watch out, Bitsy!" Garrett yelled.

I turned just in time to catch Trooper's paw across my left cheek as he jumped up on my frilly, white dress. "Trooper!" I raised my arms to push him off, but his nails scraped across my damaged elbow.

Mr. Ed grabbed the dog by the collar and yelled in his face. "Down!"

Trooper plopped down.

"Bitsy, I'm so sorry," Mr. Ed said. "Are you okay?"

I touched my cheek but didn't feel any blood. "I think so." I inspected my elbows and found the left one dripping—right down the front of my fancy dress. "Grief! Where's the bathroom?"

Ellie took my other arm. "I'll show you. Come on, Bernie."

They walked and I stumbled across the uneven dirt toward the bathroom. We waved at Ricky as he handed out programs, but he just looked down at the ground and laughed.

I was sweating by the time we got to the bathroom. The girls worked on the dress while I studied my reflection in the mirror. Although my face wasn't bleeding, it now had a bright red scratch across it.

Ellie threw the paper towel in the trash. "I'm sorry, but this blood's not coming out of your dress, and neither is the dirt from Trooper."

"Forget it," I said. "It's not going to make a bit of difference at this point."

We cleaned my elbow, did the best we could with the dress, and headed out the bathroom door, crashing into Camden and Darcy.

"Excuse me." Darcy did a double take. "Bitsy? Is that you? What happened to your hair?"

I faked a smile. "Of course it's me. It's my costume for the talent show."

"You're in the show? Oh, you're going to be great." She slapped at my bad arm. "You look so funny!"

I winced and turned away from her before she could do any more damage. "Thanks. Sorry to run, but I've got to get back out there. Don't want to be late." I walked out, with Ellie and Bernie close behind me.

"You handled that well," Ellie said.

I leaned against the wall and bent over to straighten my shoe, my orange curls falling into my face. "As far as it depends on me. . . ."

Ellie joined in and we completed the Bible verse in unison. ". . . I will live at peace with everyone."

We saw Mrs. Lyles and a bunch of other kids from church, and I just waved like I didn't have a care in the world. After all, it wasn't Bitsy Burroughs who was waving; it was an actress, and a very good one at that.

By the time we got back to the family, it was time for me to line up for the talent show. Mrs. Price gave me a kiss on the cheek, and everybody else gave me a hug. Then I braced myself to face the worst day of my life.

CHAPTER · 25

SINCE I DIDN'T KNOW ANY OF THE OTHER PARTICIPANTS, I just walked around the alcove, reading the boring, outdated notices posted on the bulletin board. Then I remembered the pictures. I skimmed the board and quickly found them. Nestled in the middle of matching T-shirts and running shorts, Ricky was the only one in white coveralls. At least he wore the team's white bandana.

Then something caught my eye, and I leaned in for a closer look. I reached up, removed the thumbtack, and brought the picture down into better focus . . . and my heart started pounding.

Still clutching the picture, I ran from the alcove and scanned the crowd for Ricky. *There he is—still handing out programs!* I tried to run to him, but something was holding me back. I tried again.

R-r-r-i-i-p-p! A huge tear appeared in the lace of my silly white dress. Jerking the dress from the nail, I hobbled to Ricky, my ankles twisting and turning in the fancy shoes.

"Ricky!"

He looked up at me and smiled. I grabbed the sleeve of his white coveralls and shoved the picture in his face.

"Ricky, look! Right there—what's on your bandana?"

He slowly took the photo from my hands, pointed, and smiled again. "That's me! That's me at Special Olympics!"

I could tell this wasn't going to be easy. "Yes, it's you. Can you tell me what's on those bandanas?"

"I won a ribbon."

"I know, Ricky, but listen, this is very important." I pointed at the corner of the bandana. "What's that?"

"I lost mine." His lip crinkled up like he was going to cry. "I can't find it."

"Well, you know what, Ricky, I might be able to help you find it. Do you remember if it had something written on it?"

He wiped his eyes. "You'll help me find it? The one with the 'S' and the 'O'? I really, really need it."

I couldn't believe what I was hearing. "Yes! Yes! I know where it is, Ricky. But why did your bandana have 'S. O.' on it?"

He laughed. "You're teasing me, right?"

"No, I'm not. I need to know."

"For Special Olympics, silly. You know that." He smiled.

Special Olympics!

Then he frowned and said, "But I lost it because I had to go to the doctor."

I tried to clear my head. "What?"

"I told the doctor I had to sweep that day, but he said I had to see him. I don't like to clean the headstones at night. It was dark. I lost my bandana."

"Are you talking about the St. Michael's cemetery? Is that where you sweep?"

"Oh, yes! Every week I do a good job. But I don't like the dark."

It was starting to make sense. "Ricky, this is important. Did you clean the graves last Wednesday night?"

"Yeah, Wednesday night. I need my bandana to keep the dust out of my mouth. I didn't like to sweep in the dark. The ghosts were screaming."

"Ricky, it wasn't ghosts. It was us! We were screaming because we thought you were a ghost! But what did you have in your hand?"

"You're being silly again, aren't you? How could I sweep the headstones without a broom?"

"BITSY! YOU'RE UP NEXT!" the director called across the walkway.

"Look, Ricky, I have to go."

"Can I go with you and get my bandana?"

I started for the alcove, but Ricky stayed right beside me. "Not right now," I said. "I have to get onstage."

"BITSY, COME ON!"

"I'M COMING!" I tried to walk faster in the high heels, tripping over clumps of dirt and rocks. I reached the alcove, Ricky still at my side. "I'm ready," I said to the director.

"It's about time." She gave me a closer inspection and wrinkled her nose. "Great makeup," she said, marking her clipboard as she walked away.

I put my foot on the bottom step, ran my fingers through my orange hair, and tried to fold the torn lace under my hem. I took a deep breath.

"Thank you," Ricky said.

"You're welcome."

The microphone crackled. "Next, we have a young lady all the way from South Carolina . . ."

"Can I get my bandana now?"

"Not now, I'm sorry."

". . . singing and dancing to the Broadway tune 'I Enjoy Being a Girl . . .' "

"I hope it weren't no problem."

I jerked around to face Ricky. "What did you say?"

"I said thank you for finding my bandana."

". . . Miss Bitsy Burroughs! . . ."

"No, after that!"

"I said, 'Can I get it now?' "

". . . Let's welcome Miss Bitsy Burroughs! . . ."

"No—after that!"

The director rushed over. "Bitsy, what's wrong? Get up there!"

Ricky shrugged. "I said, 'I hope it weren't no trouble.'"

And then I knew—it was Ricky we'd heard on the monitor.

". . . Uh, from South Carolina . . ."

I put my hands on Ricky's shoulders. "Listen. I need you to find Mr. Ed and Mrs. Price and bring them here. Can you do that, please?" I started up the steps.

"I will. I like to help people."

". . . Let's hear it for Miss Bitsy Burroughs!"

By the time I reached the top step, I knew whose voices we'd heard on the baby monitor. I turned back to watch Ricky . . . and tripped on the last step to the stage.

My performance went downhill from there. It was the longest four minutes of my life.

I don't know which was worse, the broken shoe, the tangled knot of feather boa, or the final curtsy that ended with a fall flat on my face. It didn't help that the audience laughed the whole time, especially when I pointed to my face and sang, "When boys say I'm cute and funny. . . ."

It was definitely a lesson in humility.

The crowd was still laughing and clapping as I limped down the steps. Mr. Ed and Ricky took my hands and helped me to the ground.

Mrs. Price was beaming. "Bitsy, that was a wonderful performance. I'm so proud of you!"

Nicolas wrapped himself around one sore knee while Trooper's tail swatted against the other.

Mrs. Lyles came up and gave me a hug. "Good job, Bitsy."

"Thanks, but—"

The director ran over before I could say another word. "You were terrific, honey—just terrific!" She laughed and walked back toward the stage.

I mumbled a thank-you and faced Ricky. "I need to ask you something very important. Did Mr. Norman send you to look for a picture at Mr. Hawkins's house?"

Ricky stared at the ground and whispered, "I can't mention it."

"I knew it!" I faced the adults. "I think Mr. Norman's the one who's been causing all the trouble."

The two ladies looked at each other, then at me.

"What?" Ellie's mom said.

Mr. Ed rubbed his chin. "So, what makes you think it's Norman?"

"The lies, for one thing," I replied. "He told one person he'd only visited the island once, but he told us he'd seen lots of ghosts on the island, many times—including one at Mr. Hawkins's house. He told Mr. Shorty he'd never been here at all, that he only came for the auction. Then he bought that picture for Mr. Shorty and disappeared."

Mrs. Price picked up Nicolas and said, "That does sound suspicious."

Mr. Ed took a deep breath. "She's got a point there. Nobody's seen him since the auction last night."

"I have some other ideas, too," I said, "but I need to check something out at the Pogy Plant first."

Ellie's mom patted Nicolas's back. "The Pogy Plant?"

"Yes, ma'am. Could you take me over there? It wouldn't take but a minute."

Mrs. Lyles put her hand on Mrs. Price's arm. "Look, why don't I watch the kids, and you and Ed take Bitsy over?"

"That'll work," Mr. Ed said.

Mrs. Lyles took Nicolas from Ellie's mom. "Go ahead. I'll take the kids to my house if you're not back by the time this is over."

Mr. Ed motioned to Mrs. Price and me. "Come on. We'll take my truck." Then he stopped and turned back to Mrs. Lyles. "Why don't you call the chief and ask him to meet us over there . . . just in case."

"Good idea," she said.

I took off before they had a chance to change their minds. If there's anything worse than running in heels, it's running in broken ones.

CHAPTER · 26

TROOPER AND I SAT IN THE MIDDLE AS WE BOUNCED our way to the Pogy Plant. Within minutes, Mr. Ed drove the truck through the gate and pulled up beside Mr. Johnny's building. He cut the ignition.

"Here we are," Mr. Ed said. "But we'd better hurry. Looks like it's about to rain."

"This won't take long," I said. "I just need to check the trash on the path."

Mrs. Price opened her door. "The trash?"

Trooper jumped over me and pushed Ellie's mom out of the way. He took off.

"Yes, ma'am. I'll be right back." I left the truck and followed the dog. I wished I had my tennis shoes.

Trooper sprinted to the water's edge and stopped, but I took my time. Carefully placing one foot in front of the other, I searched the pathway, hoping for that one piece of litter, that one clue that could prove my suspicion.

Thunder rumbled a warning, and the sky swirled into a gray mass of dark clouds.

"Hurry up, Bitsy," Mr. Ed yelled. "The storm's coming."

"Just one more minute. I'm almost—"

And then I saw it. The Teaberry gum wrapper was exactly where it had been Thursday night. I knelt down as the first huge drops of rain spattered around me.

Trooper growled. I looked up to see the tugboat bouncing in the rippling water.

Ka-boom! The thunder crashed the same instant the lightning bolt split an enormous oak tree at the edge of the water. A man's shriek echoed through the air.

I tried to stand to my high-heeled feet but couldn't keep my balance, so I crawled on my wounded knees toward the truck. Another duet of thunder and lightning danced around me, followed by another shriek—coming from the tugboat!

Mr. Ed ran toward me, lost his footing, and landed hard on the muddy path.

"Did you hear that?" I yelled.

Before he could answer, the tugboat roared to life and Trooper announced a new warning. There was Mr. Norman, jumping from the boat and disconnecting the chain from the metal post. The black dog lunged for the bad guy's leg, and Mr. Norman screamed again, this time in pain. Then he broke away from Trooper.

Mr. Ed grabbed my arm. "Get back to the truck!"

He scrambled to his feet and took off for the boat, but Mr. Norman was too quick. The tug inched out of the cove and headed toward open water.

The rain stopped as quickly as it started. Mrs. Price ran up behind me and covered me in a bear hug. "Oh, Bitsy, are you okay?"

"Yes, ma'am. Just a little wet."

Suddenly, Mr. Bill was beside us. "The chief just called," he yelled to Mr. Ed. "They're on their way."

"Mr. Bill," I said, pointing to the orange crane yawning at the river, "does that thing work?"

"Of course it does."

"Could it stop a tugboat?"

He paused, and then his eyes lit up. "I don't know, but we'll sure try!" He climbed up the muddy steps and brought the crane to life. Working the hand controls, he maneuvered the giant hook toward the getaway boat.

Mr. Ed came up, wiping his face with a soggy handkerchief. "Is he trying to do what I think he's trying to do?"

I nodded.

"I bet it'd work if the tugboat didn't have any juice." Within seconds the engine sputtered, coughed, and breathed its last. Mr. Ed looked up at the clearing sky. "Wow. Thanks."

Word must have spread quickly at the talent show, because the crowd grew as Mr. Bill worked the swinging hook back and forth, back and forth, closer and closer to the drifting tugboat. Ellie's mom kept her arm around my shoulders while I held my breath, my heart thumping in my chest.

The hook crouched over the rusty heap. With a loud *boof,* the line dropped and bounced—and barely missed its mark. Murmurs rumbled through the gathering mob.

The crane operator raised the weapon again, fixed it over the rusty tugboat, and waited. Seconds passed as the hook circled lazily above.

"Get him!" someone shouted, but the crane didn't move. The crowd was silent as Mr. Bill moved his hands this way, then that, jerking the controls like giant joysticks. Without warning, the hook dropped on its target and snared the tugboat!

The onlookers cheered and clapped as the crane pulled the boat to shore.

"He's getting away!" someone shouted from the crowd.

We looked up to see Mr. Norman, bouncing in the ripple, trying to swim out into open water.

Trooper paced on the riverbank for a moment, barked fiercely, then dove into the water. Mr. Norman tried to fight off the determined dog, but within seconds, Trooper had him. The policemen arrived in time to pull the bad guy to shore.

Fog as thick as cotton candy rolled in from the river

as the officers, with Mr. Norman handcuffed between them, turned around and faced the crowd. Trooper, the retired police dog, led the way up the path to the waiting car.

The policeman monitoring the crowd held up his hands and called for silence. "Okay, you can all go home now. We'll take it from here."

I started back to the truck, but he stopped me. "All except you, miss. We need to talk."

"Sir?" I croaked.

Mrs. Price squeezed my shoulder. "Don't worry. I'm not going anywhere."

"Where's Mr. Norman?" We turned around to see Ricky, his eyes wide. "I think Mr. Norman needs me. I like to help people."

Mr. Ed patted Ricky on the back. "Don't worry, son. Norman's going to get a lot of help where he's going."

Ricky pushed through to the front of the crowd as the officers approached with their suspect. "I didn't mention it, Mr. Norman. I didn't mention it."

The bad guy never missed a beat. "Whatever."

CHAPTER · 27

IT WAS PAST TEN O'CLOCK, BUT NONE OF US WERE sleepy. Ellie handed me a cold IBC Root Beer and squeezed beside me in the recliner. "So, how did you know Mr. Norman would be at the Pogy Plant?"

"I didn't know—it surprised me as much as anybody. I only went back there to look for the Teaberry gum wrapper. I thought I'd seen it Thursday night when we walked down to the tugboat, before we saw the Pogy Witch Woman. I knew if it was there, then Mr. Norman probably was the one who dropped it. I mean, after all, how many people do you know who chew Teaberry gum?" I took a swallow of root beer. "It proved he had the opportunity to scare us with the light in the woods."

Garrett grinned and said, "There you go again, sounding like a detective."

Ernie stretched. "You've got a point, but how did he know we were going to be there Thursday night?"

Am I the only one who pays attention to this stuff? I wondered. "Because of what you said at Shorty's. Remember? When we were sitting on the sidewalk talking to Mr. Norman? You said we should go to the Pogy Plant that night and check it out." I poked him in the chest. "So that one's your fault."

Bernie moved to the arm of the recliner. "What else? What else gave him away?"

"Well, remember when he said he owned a Circuit Shack in St. Augustine?"

Everybody nodded their heads.

"I figured that if he owned a Circuit Shack, he would know how to use a DVD player to fake a ghost, right?"

"Yes, I guess so," Bernie said.

"And some of the phrases he said gave him away, too. Like 'whatever' and 'don't mention it.'"

"Did Ricky have anything to do with it?" Garrett asked.

"Nope," I said. "He was only trying to be helpful. He had no idea he was helping a bad guy."

Mr. Price walked into the living room and set a bowl of popcorn on the coffee table. "Say, Bitsy, you ended up having a pretty exciting day, didn't you? I can't believe I had to work and miss all the fun."

I squeezed out of the recliner and grabbed a handful of popcorn. "I wouldn't exactly call it fun, but it was definitely exciting."

"Well, there's more. The police chief just called. Looks like this isn't the first time Norman's been in trouble. He had two outstanding warrants in Georgia."

That didn't surprise me at all. "Wow. He really is a bad guy. Did the police find out what he was up to here?"

"Yes. First of all, Norman never owned a Circuit Shack, he just worked at one in Jacksonville. And you were right, Bitsy. He was trying to scare the community into not supporting the resource center."

Ellie draped herself over one arm of the recliner. "Why would he do that, Daddy?"

"Because he wanted the picture."

Bernie stood, her mouth hanging open. "You mean Mr. Shorty's picture? The one we took?"

"Yes. Remember I told you Norman worked at Circuit Shack? Well, Mr. Hawkins had been having some trouble with kids ringing his doorbell and running off."

Bernie sucked in a big breath and covered her mouth. Ernie just stared at his sister.

"He was real concerned about it," Mr. Price continued, "so his lawyer told him if he was that concerned, he should get a security system. The lawyer had no idea he'd really do it, but he called Circuit Shack about putting in a video camera. They sent Norman."

"I knew he'd been here before!" I said.

"Anyway, Norman was putting a tiny camera on the frame of Shorty's picture because it had a direct shot of the front door window. While Norman was fiddling with the portrait, he discovered a bunch of money hidden between the picture and the frame. Mr. Hawkins walked in, saw Norman messing with the picture, and said he'd changed his mind about getting a security system. Norman pretended he hadn't seen the money, and planned to go back and steal it a few days later. But on the way home that night, he was in a terrible car wreck. Messed his legs up really bad. Then, while he was in the hospital, Mr. Hawkins died. Norman apparently heard about the auction and was determined to get well in time to get the picture . . . and the money."

"That explains his limp," Ellie said.

Something still didn't seem right to me. "But couldn't he have just stolen the picture when he broke in to set up the fake ghost? It would have been a lot easier."

"Um, I can answer that one," Bernie said. "The picture wasn't there. It was riding around in the back of our car."

It was Garrett's turn. "But why did he keep trying to use a ghost to scare everybody when the picture was already gone? That doesn't make sense."

Mr. Price propped his feet on the coffee table. "He told the police he thought the picture was still inside the house somewhere, and the best way to keep buyers away was to make people think the house was haunted. He figured Shorty would try to get someone to bid on it for him, so he offered to do it. Of course, Norman didn't really care about Shorty and the picture. He just wanted to grab the money and get out of town."

"So how much money was there?" Garrett asked.

"The chief said about $10,000."

"Ten thousand dollars?" I yelled. "Why'd Mr. Hawkins have that kind of money at his house?"

"That's actually very common for people his age. They'd been through the Great Depression, where families lost everything they had because the banks went out of business. They didn't trust banks anymore, so they hid their money in mattresses or jelly jars."

Ernie leaned toward Bernie. "Just think, there was $10,000 riding in the back of Aunt Myrna's car, and we didn't know it."

Mr. Price laughed. "Well, actually the money wasn't behind the picture, after all."

That got my attention. "You mean after all that trouble, he didn't even get the money? Serves him right."

"But what happened to it?" Ellie asked her daddy.

"Well, I guess Mr. Hawkins moved it after he saw Norman messing with the picture. After Norman told his story to the police, they checked the house and found the money in a box of books—a box no one even bid on at the auction."

"So that $10,000 still belongs to the resource center?" I asked.

Mr. Price nodded.

"Cool!"

"Did Mr. Shorty know about the money?" Ernie asked.

"No," Mr. Price said. "He's totally innocent. He just wanted that picture with his mother in it."

I plopped on the couch beside Mr. Price and added my feet to the coffee table. "Wow, what a story."

Ding-dong.

I wondered who would be ringing the doorbell so late at night. Mr. Price got up and opened the door. A microphone appeared in front of his face.

"Is Bitsy Burroughs here? Could we see her?" A pretty woman poked her head in the door and then barged into the living room, her microphone cord snaking along behind her. "So, which one of you is Bitsy?" she asked, her teeth filling her face.

I ran my fingers through my orange hair, stretched my shorts over my crusty knees, and smiled. "I am."

The phone rang in the kitchen. *Don't people ever sleep around here?* I wondered.

"Well, young lady, you've had a busy day!" the teeth lady said.

For the first time, I noticed a man with a TV camera. *A red light really does glow when the camera's on!* "Yes, ma'am," I said. The lady waited, but I didn't say anything else. I just stood there like a doofus.

Mr. Price stepped between the lady and me. "Excuse me, but may I help you?"

I leaned around him and smiled at the camera with the red light.

The lady filled her face with teeth again. "I'm sorry. I just wanted to speak to the Amelia Island hero."

I smiled at the camera.

Mrs. Price called from the hallway, "Bitsy, can you—" She came into the living room. "Oh, excuse me. Hey, aren't you from Channel Twelve News?"

"Yes, I just wanted a few words from our hero here."

Mrs. Price walked over and draped her arm around me. She straightened her hair, faced the camera, and smiled. "Well, you'll be the first to know—Bitsy's not only the hero of the day, but she's also the first-place winner of the Amelia Island July Fourth Talent Show!"

I forgot about the camera and turned to Ellie's mom. "I won? I really won?"

Mrs. Price didn't look at me at all. She just kept her arm around my shoulders and stared at the camera. "Yes, Bitsy. You won."

I faced the camera, brushed back my orange hair, and smiled. "Cool."

CHAPTER · 28

WELL, THINGS TURNED OUT ALL RIGHT ON AMELIA Island. Not only did the committee get to keep the money for the resource center, but after everyone realized the "ghost" was really Mr. Norman, they supported the center with their own money, too.

The talent show judges said I won because I was the funniest comedy act they'd ever seen. I didn't tell them any different.

After paying Mrs. Price the ten dollars I owed her, I still had ninety dollars prize money. I didn't know where the other ten dollars was going to come from for camp, but I was pretty sure my parents would scrounge it up from somewhere. They did.

But the best part about being on Amelia Island was something I learned while I was there. I learned that the best things in life really and truly are free. And I also learned that the best things in life . . . aren't even things at all.

ALSO BY VONDA SKINNER SKELTON

Bitsy and the Mystery at Tybee Island

When Bitsy convinces her parents to let her favorite cousin, Matt, tag along on a rare family vacation, adventure isn't the only thing they find. Pirates in the cove, buried treasure, a skeleton on the beach, and a mysterious stranger are a few of the secrets hidden on Tybee Island. Shortly after their arrival, Bitsy and Matt are given a stern warning to stay out of a dark, abandoned fort on the island. Is it because valuable jewels really are hidden inside, or is someone afraid the two will discover more than just buried treasure? When Bitsy and Matt disregard the warning and explore the fort anyway, Bitsy learns a lesson about the importance of family and discovers that friends can be found in the most unexpected places.

Hardback ISBN 1-57072-253-6 / $23.95 • Trade Paper ISBN 1-57072-254-4 / $13.95

You can learn more about Bitsy and her friends, enter cool contests, and talk with the author! Just ask your parents if you can visit

www.vondaskelton.com